ALSO AVAILABLE IN LAUREL-LEAF BOOKS:

HOOPS, *Walter Dean Myers*
WHIRLIGIG, *Paul Fleischman*
HEROES, *Robert Cormier*
TUNES FOR BEARS TO DANCE TO, *Robert Cormier*
BREAKING BOXES, *A. M. Jenkins*
THE KILLER'S COUSIN, *Nancy Werlin*
FOR MIKE, *Shelley Sykes*
HOLES, *Louis Sachar*
HATE YOU, *Graham McNamee*
CLOSE TO A KILLER, *Marsha Qualey*

REMEMBERING THE GOOD TIMES

Richard Peck

Published by
Bantam Doubleday Dell Books for Young Readers
a division of
Bantam Doubleday Dell Publishing Group, Inc.
1540 Broadway
New York, New York 10036

ISBN: 0-440-97339-2

RL: 4.9

Reprinted by arrangement with Delacorte Press

Printed in the United States of America

April 1986
 OPM 33 32 31 30 29 28 27 26 25 24

for the Majers:
Diane and Gerry,
Emily, Carrie, and Oliver

REMEMBERING
THE GOOD TIMES

CHAPTER ONE

Trav and I almost argued once about which one of us got to Kate first. I did. I remember the day, almost the minute we met. We were still kids—twelve, so it was nearly four years ago. A lifetime.

I was still living with my mom, but my dad had me sometimes on weekends, here in the mobile home. "What I got out of my divorce," he used to say, "is a full-time trailer and a part-time kid."

He had a hookup behind the service station on the truck route into the city, which was about the only paved road around at that time. It was pretty fringy territory in those days, with roadside stands selling melons and Indian corn in the fall, and real ditches full of ragweed and goldenrod and all kinds of things that grew because they wanted to.

It was still open country. You could even hunt some of it, but they were grading back in the fields for the new subdivisions and excavating for the big IBM headquarters building and adding on to the school.

That's why Dad came over here: because he works construction.

The station we were behind was at the intersection of the truck route and a county road. It wasn't as bad as it sounds, and Dad was good friends with Scotty MacDowell who ran the station, Scotty's Sunoco.

A horse farm ran along one side of the county road. They gave pony rides and lessons and boarded horses. I don't even know who ran the place. It's long gone now.

Across the county road from the horse farm was a big orchard behind us that had definitely seen better days. It was pear trees because of the clay soil, and really jungly. You needed to chop your way through some of it with a machete. I was starting to explore around in there one Saturday afternoon when I met this girl.

She was coming through the orchard rows at an angle, which is the hard way to do it, but she knew where she was going. I heard her—somebody way off, but the trees were leafed out. So I waited along one of the rows, expecting to see somebody cross ahead of me. Instead, she lifted a limb next to my ear and there she was, wearing sneakers, shorts, a tank top. She was fairly flat-chested and a little taller than me, so I figured we were the same age.

She just glanced at me like this was no big surprise. Besides, she was in a hurry. She was busy all the time, even back then. "Do you want to see a foal being born?"

I didn't know, but she moved out. "Come on." I

followed her out of the orchard, stepping where she stepped.

"How do you know it's happening?" We were across the road and out of the ditch. She'd hooked one skinny brown leg over the horse-farm fence.

"I heard the mare," she said, swinging over.

She was striding across the barn lot, sending up spurts of dust. Then we were both leaning over the half door and looking into the barn, and it was all happening. The vet was there with a couple of the farmhands, too involved to care if we watched or not.

They were standing clear, letting the mare, a big red one, find the place she wanted to be. She settled into a pile of straw, stretched out on her side. Her taped-up tail was switched back, and you could see something. Coming out of her was just a little swell of membrane, a wet balloon. Then this miniature hoof broke through it, and we saw that too. It was covered with mossy stuff.

"That's to protect the mare's womb from getting cut." The girl watched, knowing already. She'd been here before.

Right away another hoof pushed out, and now the mare was really beginning to work. You could see her coat ripple from the muscles working underneath. She made some noise, nothing much.

Right behind the feet the foal's head appeared, soapy and sleek with its ears laid back. "Now she's got to get busy," the girl said. Her elbows were propped up on the door. "This is going to be the hard part—the foal's shoulders and withers."

The mare thrashed a little, and her muscles flickered down her, but it was over in about a minute. The slippery foal's body slid out right into the arms of the vet, who was squatting there for it. The mare threw her head around, rolling her eyes, scattering straw. She snorted but got calm, because it was over for her. Just realizing what happened, she jerked her head back and looked past herself at the foal.

It was a colt with its ears plastered back, very still. I was afraid it was dead, but then, without moving, it let out with a little high whinny. The girl beside me relaxed. Her chin was on her hands and she was grinning.

The colt looked around, somewhat surprised. He twitched his ears, and they stood up from his head. He had a stubby little mane like a damp brush. The mare was watching, but she turned away and began to pull herself up. The colt's hind feet weren't quite born yet, but then they fell free. She rounded on him, checked him out with her nose, licked at his coat. The miracle of birth. I hung on the barn door, sort of stunned.

"It'll take a while for the colt to find his feet," the girl said, still watching. "Want to wait?"

I had no plans.

The thing I noticed was how little there was for the vet to do. The mare took charge, cleaning up the colt, making big tongue patterns in his coat. He was her color, her son. She gave him little nose-nudges, just to let him know who she was, I guess.

A long time later he decided to try standing up. His

legs were wild and wobbly and like stilts for him. He couldn't get them sorted out. Then suddenly it worked. He was up, this little knife-narrow body on these spindly knob-kneed legs. He looked a long way down at his front feet and then around at the world. Then he took a step toward the mare and began to feed at her nipple.

"How'd he get all that figured out so quick?" I said to the girl. I was truly amazed.

"He just did." She brought her shoulders up in a shrug. "Let's go," she said. "There's going to be after-birth, and it's gross."

We were back in the orchard when she said over her shoulder, "Want to see a snake hole?"

Horses, yes. Snakes, no.

I couldn't say that, but she seemed to hear me holding off. She turned around and looked me over. I wasn't much to look at in those days, but she saw all there was. "Well?" she said.

"You want to get a bottle of pop at the Sunoco?" I said. "I'll pay."

There were little sweat beads on her upper lip. She had gray eyes that took everything in and eyebrows so fine they almost weren't there. If I hadn't been twelve, I'd have seen how great-looking she was going to be. She wiped the sweat away with the back of her hand. "Might take you up on that. What do they call you?"

"Buck Mendenhall."

She stared. I guess the name didn't fit me too well. "I'm Kate Lucas. I live over there." I didn't see a house back where she jerked her thumb. Maybe I noticed a little clearing in the trees, maybe not. "You?"

"I live down at the Sunoco."

"With Scotty and Irene?" She looked puzzled.

Irene and Scotty lived upstairs over the station in the old cinder-block story-and-a-half structure.

"No, my dad lives behind them in the tr—mobile home."

"And you too?" She was checking me out before she made any moves.

"He gets me on weekends usually. The rest of the time I'm with my mom over at Farnham, which is—"

"I know where Farnham is. Okay. I never knew anybody who lived in a trailer. Can we see inside?"

So we headed off down the orchard, and I had to show her what the inside of a trailer looks like.

It's hooked up on a pad right behind Irene's vegetable garden, a rusty-chrome Clarion make, not even a double-wide. It has concrete blocks up to the door, and it's built in below for insulation and anchored in case of tornadoes. Inside, Kate checked out everything. Not that there's much, but every inch has to count. There's an all-purpose room at one end with a kitchenette along one side. Then a hallway next to a basic bathroom. At the far end is Dad's room, which is the size of a small truck bed. In fact, his bed takes up about all the space. Even at that, his feet stick out at the end. You can't open the bedroom door without slamming his soles. The door was shut that afternoon.

Dad slept a lot after he and Mom split up, which I didn't think too much about.

But Kate saw everything else, checking out shelves and the bathroom, which seemed really interesting to her.

"You can use it if you need to," I said, which was my idea of manners at the time.

In the kitchenette she ran her hands along the unit that combines the burners and oven and under-the-counter refrigerator. "It's like a walnut. Everything fits," she said. "Where do you sleep?"

I showed her how the table folds up and the Hide-A-Bed pulls out, and you can't move in the room till you put it back. Then we went around to the front of the station for pop.

I never had to pay, and it didn't come out of a machine. There was this big old red steel vat, an antique. You lifted the lid, and the pop bottles were bobbing around in a big bath of melting ice. Those things should never have gone out of style. On a hot day you could stick your whole arm in that ice water —both arms if you wanted to. We fished out a couple of colas and hunkered down on the hot curb in front of the station. Kate hitched her tank top out of her shorts and wiped the mouth of the bottle with it. I wasn't wearing a shirt, so I just tipped back the bottle and drank, which I probably figured was more macho anyhow.

Scotty was in the service area with a car up on the lift, and maybe he had some Saturday help. We could hear him in there, dropping tools and singing under somebody's oil pan. I wasn't old enough to be much help to him, but my arms were getting long, so I could clean windshields. It's funny how much you want to work before you're old enough to hold a job.

What did Kate and I talk about? Not the mare foaling, I'm pretty sure. There was something sacred about that. I know we discovered we were both just out of sixth grade and had junior high staring us in the face.

Personally, I was pretty nervous about that. You heard things about junior high, what a big tough place it was. You heard they had lockers, and you had to memorize your combination. And for every different subject, a different teacher, and they were all vicious graders. You heard that the seventh-grade class was the lowest of the low. Worse than dirt.

We probably talked about that, though I can't picture Kate being too worried. I do remember the sun had bleached her hair, and she'd chopped it off for the hot weather and tucked it behind her ears. She had chigger bites on her legs, and you could smell the turpentine she'd put on them. We didn't start up a friendship that summer. We were either a little too old or a little too young for that. I only saw her twice, that time and once more.

It was a few weeks later, because Irene's first tomatoes were ready for picking. Those Saturday evenings were all about the same. There was an outside stairway up behind the station to Irene and Scotty's apartment. Scotty and Dad would sit out on the steps, drinking a couple cans of Coors, and Scotty would sing. He looked like a somewhat battered teddy bear, and he wouldn't have minded being Mac Davis.

Even for an adult, he had absolutely no ear for music, and he had a guitar that wasn't even electric. He knew three chords, but nothing stopped him when he got going: "Wichita Lineman" and "Worried Man Blues" and "That's All She Wrote" and "Wildwood Flower" and a song I still swear he made up called "Heart as Big as a Fruehauf Trailer Truck."

I remember those long evenings and Scotty's three chords drifting off over the orchard. If the bugs weren't biting, Irene worked her garden, bending along the rows and making neat, evening-colored piles of the weeds. She had a way with tomatoes, which she trained way up high on stakes. They were prizewinners, big monster beefsteaks, red as blood. You could make a meal out of them.

Irene was a real quiet woman, tall and sort of gaunt. Older than Scotty, maybe; I wasn't sure. One night she said, "Buck, skin up the road to Mrs. Prior's and give her this bucket of tomatoes. She's that first lane on your left past the orchard."

I found the lane and the house standing way back. It was a real farmhouse with a lightning rod. The front porch was glassed in, and there were three windows above, with only a dim light in one of them.

I crunched along the lane around to the back. Whoever goes up to the front door of a farmhouse? On the big back porch stood a rusted-out thing, a cream separator, but I didn't know what it was. Nobody seemed to be around when I went up on the porch to leave the tomatoes.

Maybe I just noticed a little glint of something steely there past the separator. Then this voice, loud, filling the universe:

"Heyboy, what business have you got here anyway?"

Every hair on my head stood up. Even my feet freaked out, and I couldn't move.

Something was sliding out from around the separator. I saw the glitter of spoke wheels. It was a wheelchair, and it kept coming on, making no sound. There was an old woman in it; I mean *old*. Her hands on the wheels were blue-white, and her glasses were like two moons. She really loomed up.

"I say what business have you got on my porch?"

My voice was beginning to change, but hers was cracking in every direction. It was like she was talking into a pan: real hollow.

"Tomatoes. Irene told me to bring some." I held one up for proof. I'd been setting them out on the floor to take the bucket back. "They're for you if you're Mrs. Prior."

"As if you didn't know," she said. "You the same boy who broke out my shed windows? I bet a nickel you are."

"No, ma'am."

She rolled to a stop and put her hands in her lap. The fingers were all crooked. It was a warm evening, but she had a quilt over her knees and something around her shoulders.

I hadn't moved, and she was close. Then she leaned forward in the wheelchair. I thought she might come flying out. She could have flown up into a tree and it wouldn't have surprised me.

We were about nose to nose, and my knees were locked. I had the bucket handle in a death grip. Right in my face, almost whispering, she said, "You want to know the first president I can remember? I'm talkin' presidents of the United States."

"Okay. I mean, yes, ma'am."

She seemed to have a little drawstring on her mouth, pulled tight in a million wrinkles.

"William McKinley."

I'd have believed Lincoln.

"And he was shot dead in nineteen hundred and one. Of course, I was just a tyke at the time, but still . . ."

Her finger came up then, bent in about six places, and she sighted along it at me. "I'm the third oldest woman in Slocum Township. But when it comes to meanness, I'm Number One." Her finger pointed up to the porch roof. "I'm too mean to die."

The lightning bugs were out, dull sparks in the night. Then there was a shape at the back door.

"Polly," someone said through the screen, "are you talking to yourself again?"

"Might as well be," the old lady said, and Kate stepped out onto the porch.

She was the same Kate, but the dark softened her chopped-off hair and made her look taller and even thinner. She walked over and ran her hand along the back of the wheelchair.

"You got yourself a caller, Katie," the old lady said. "I bet a nickel he's sweet on you. Looky there, he brought you a mess of tomatoes." She sat back in the chair to feel Kate's arm behind her and to watch me squirm.

"Ah . . . no. It was Irene, she said—"

"Hi, Buck," Kate said.

"I knew you knew him." The old lady nodded. "Boys is going to be thicker around here than speck eyes on a potato. I'll have to clean my shotgun."

"This is Polly Prior," Kate said to me. "She's my great-grandmother, Buck."

"Oh, boy, am I old," said Polly Prior. "I was lucky they didn't wing me when they shot McKinley."

"My mother and I live with her. It's Polly's house and her orchard."

"So watch your step," said Polly Prior.

I was sort of confused. At that age any little thing will throw you off. I started climbing backwards down the steps, dragging the bucket.

"I've got to get Polly to bed," Kate said.

"What for?" Polly said. "I don't sleep."

But I was backing out of it by then, and Kate was wedging the screen door open to get the wheelchair inside.

"Tell Irene thanks for the tomatoes," she said over her shoulder.

I noticed how Kate's hands fitted the rubber grips

on the wheelchair handles, firm and gentle and not particularly like a kid. Efficient. I noticed that.

I saw Kate. First.

Then, because life keeps springing these big surprises on you and because my mom married Fred Wunderlich, I met up with Kate again, and we both met Trav.

CHAPTER TWO

It took us another year to get together because I went through seventh grade in Farnham, forty-five miles away. Over there, junior high wasn't the big leap I worried about, mainly because I knew everybody anyway.

Mom and Dad had to sell the house after they split up, so she and I were living in an apartment, the cardboard condo. What with one thing and another, it was a pretty long year. Nothing much changed but my voice.

I missed a few weekends with Dad, too, sometimes because of the weather and sometimes because he was getting a lot of overtime. Mom said she thought he might be dating, but maybe she thought that because *she* was dating.

I don't remember seeing Kate at all through that year. If Dad was working Saturday mornings, I hung around the trailer, watching *Roadrunner* and *Rubik the Amazing Cube* and *Aquaman*. At that age my brain gunned a lot in neutral.

In August on the day the divorce came through,

Mom dropped the bomb that blew me away, literally. She told me she was marrying Fred Wunderlich and we'd be moving to Cleveland. Just like that.

I had to have noticed Fred hanging around the cardboard condo. He'd been around quite a bit. But I was noticing just about what I wanted to notice, and I hadn't noticed him. The feeling appeared to be mutual.

"You can't be that surprised," Mom said.

Try *stunned*.

"There are schools in Cleveland," she said.

I could see them already. The chain-link fencing, the narc-squad German shepherds, the homemade tattoos on bulging biceps, and sudden death in the parking lot. A punk prison. While Mom was talking about a new start for both of us, I was looking at the end of the world.

It took me two weeks of steady effort, but I finally convinced Mom that a boy's best friend is his dad—his real one.

Frankly, I wasn't thinking about Dad then or even if he'd take me. All I could think of was not ending up in Cleveland with two strangers named Mr. and Mrs. Wunderlich. Dad took me. They worked it out over many phone calls. Mom used the special voice divorced people use on each other: reasonable, polite, long-distance.

So while she was packing for Cleveland, I was packing, light, for the trailer and Dad. It all happened fast, but on the day Dad was coming to get me, he was a little late. While I was waiting around the front door, getting anxious, I looked through the empty apartment to the kitchen.

Mom was out there, having a last cup of coffee in a mug she'd saved back from the packing. She looked like somebody else, a young girl, slumped there against the sink. Both her hands were on the mug, and her hair was in her eyes. She didn't make a sound, and she wasn't moving, but I knew she was crying, or very close.

I had to be out there with her, but I couldn't quite get myself through the kitchen door, so I hung there. She set the mug aside on the drainboard and ran a hand through her hair, needing a minute.

I saw something I'd never seen before. My mom was really pretty in a quiet way. She was hot and sweaty from packing, and upset. She had on a bad sweat shirt, and her hair was messy, but she was really pretty. I wish I'd told her. It wouldn't have cost a dime.

She rubbed her nose with the back of her hand exactly like Kate. "The thing is," she said, "you don't see these things coming." She wasn't looking at me. She was looking up at the clean circle on the wall where the electric clock had hung. "One thing happens and then another, and then you lose."

When she looked at me, she was more like my mom. "Who are you going to be the next time I see you?" Her voice wobbled all over the room. "You'll be changed."

"No I won't." I was looking down at my feet. I

needed a bigger sneaker size every other month. "I'll be the same."

"I'd stop the clock if I could," Mom said, "but I packed it."

Then she put her hands over her face and broke down. I guess we both did, but then I heard Dad's truck outside, and it was time to go, but I didn't run.

Two of us full-time in the trailer wasn't quite like weekends. Dad filled up the space himself without any help. He had to duck through doorways and take the little hall at an angle to accommodate his shoulders. He's a big, good-looking monster, and we did a certain amount of running into each other at first. Since he was working steady and piling up overtime, he had a plan for moving into bigger quarters, more permanent, especially after I showed up. The trailer was strictly temporary and still is.

Single-parent status was still a new concept for him, but he was anxious to get us squared away. At first we played it like weekends. But then he took me down to K Mart and bought me all new underwear. We stopped eating at Roy Rogers and started buying groceries. We began to make regular Laundromat runs. He was hustling, trying to be two parents, but I figured he'd settle down when I got into school.

Slocum Township Junior High was the second new school I'd started in two years. I was beginning to feel like a drifter. There'd always been a combined junior-senior high here, one little brick building with hardwood floors out there in a pasture. But with the new people moving into the area, they'd expanded it into a campus of schools.

The senior high got the new facilities on the other side of the ballfield and track. The junior high got stuck with the old building, which is the way the world works. But they added a classroom wing to one end of it and an activities wing to the other. Not a whole lot of thought had gone into pulling the place together, but they had a Commitment to Quality Education. It said so on a big plaque hanging over the main hall.

Easing in here for eighth grade wasn't too tense because that was the year the Greenbriar subdivisions opened. The place was full of newcomers: IBM families, kids fresh from the city, a real invasion of the Preppie People. That was also the year they closed the little Pine Hill school south of us, which was an authentic country school, with wooden construction and outhouses. So that splinter group got pulled in too.

It didn't take long to see how everybody divided into two main types. The people from Greenbriar and the other fancy new areas were called "Subs," for suburbanites. The kids who'd always lived around here naturally got called "Slos," for Slocum Township. At the bottom of this bunch were the Pine Hill people. So here we had a definite split, very visible, and it never went away. And way out in left field was the Farnham transfer group, consisting of me.

In the midst of all this, I'd catch glimpses of Kate, the only halfway-familiar face. It was Kate a year later. Her hair was long and smooth, not as blond as summer. No chigger bites that I could see. She was beginning to have a figure, which I happened to notice.

I didn't say anything to her, not being sure if she remembered. Besides, the guys stayed on one side of an invisible line, and girls stayed on the other. It's some rule of junior high nature, and I don't know what it means.

Apart from Kate, the whole place was basically a blur, and the first new face that popped out was not a pretty one. It belonged to Skeeter Calhoun. There are people who ought to be separated from society long before junior high, and Skeeter's on the short list.

He was from Pine Hill, and even the other kids from down there kept out of his way. Pine Hill's in the south end of the township, without a pine or a hill in sight. They've got a lot of plastic sheeting down there instead of storm windows, and a lot of cars parked in a lot of yards. Even when the suburbs spread that far south, they'll probably skip over it. Skeeter Calhoun was hardcore Pine Hill. Worse yet, he weighed in at about a hundred and eighty pounds and shaved.

Since the junior high facilities were either new or refurbished, the first two assemblies we had were all about respecting our new environment and protecting the taxpayers' investment. This seemed to set Skeeter off. His first achievement was to wrench the writing arm off his homeroom desk. Assigned to our

homeroom was a new teacher, Ms. Sherrie Slater.
When she noticed shirtless Skeeter Calhoun in his
bib overalls making toothpicks out of the taxpayers'
investment, she turned pale and assigned him a new
desk, quick.

However much you tried, you couldn't miss him.
He was one dumb slob in class, but he kept himself
alert. In gym class we ran a lot of laps. The coach
called them "wind sprints," but it was running laps.
We did this for half the gym period, which simplified
the entire PE program.

On wet days we ran in the gym. On dry ones we
ran out on the track. Skeeter seemed to know I didn't
quite fit either the Slo or the Sub category. He had an
instinct for people already cut out of the pack. Actually, he was a problem for everybody, and the people
he was really gunning for full-time were the weaker
teachers.

He wasn't fast, partly because he was carrying
around more weight than the rest of us. But when
we'd start running laps, we'd be bunched up in a
group, and Skeeter was right in there.

One day we were just getting up speed, when a
very hairy ankle in an ancient, high-topper basket-
ball shoe hooked out and caught my leg. It didn't
take me any time at all to grab the track with my
entire body. The school nurse spent a busy morning
picking cinders out of me.

"What happened?" Dad said that night, because
it's hard to hide that much iodine.

"Fell."

Dad cocked an eyebrow.

"Skeeter Calhoun dropped me on the track."

Dad waited.

"So I'll get my revenge in about ten years when my arms are bigger than his fingers."

"Keep your guard up when you get there," Dad said. "I think you've got a glass jaw."

Though he was trouble on the track, Skeeter was worse indoors, where he seemed to feel boxed in. Every morning he hit the place like his own strike force while the administration busily looked in other directions.

Ms. Sherrie Slater, who was going through her first year of teaching, wasn't a good choice for the junior high level. She was too young and a lot too gorgeous. The boys liked her in all the wrong ways, and the girls didn't like her at all. Teacher-training hadn't prepared her for Skeeter.

He always came in late to show her who's boss, and then he was all over the room. He just about swung from the light fixtures, and he had the arms for it. Then, when Ms. Slater was trying to take roll, he was right there behind her, writing some really inventively spelled stuff on the chalkboard.

"Skeeter, take your seat," Ms. Slater would say in this small, kind of hopeless voice, but it didn't carry to Skeeter.

I guess he was trying to find his limits, but nobody was there to set any for him. One morning he whipped around from the chalkboard and, in one massive sweep, wiped Ms. Slater's desk clean. All her

papers, books, a little glass thing with flowers in it all
went. What didn't go into the wastebasket went all
over the floor. Skeeter reached down and jerked a
desk drawer open. He grabbed Ms. Slater's purse and
shook out the contents all over. You heard round
things, lipsticks and things, rolling away.

This didn't get a thing out of his system. He'd
upped his own ante. He clomped through the mess
he'd made and down the aisle, where he dropped
into his desk with a crash. He was quivering and
working his hands, making a grunting sound. People
were scared. Ms. Slater still had her roll book in her
hands, but she was frozen in place.

In a way we were more experienced than she was.
We knew she couldn't go for help. There wouldn't be
anybody to help her anyway, and she couldn't show
herself up as a new teacher who couldn't handle
things. She couldn't run and she couldn't deal with it,
and we knew it. What Skeeter knew is anybody's
guess.

Then this guy stands up. I don't think I'd ever
noticed him before. He was a basic Sub, in a blue
broadcloth shirt and tailored pants instead of jeans.
Good haircut.

He started walking down Skeeter's aisle, slow but
not too slow. He kept coming on until he was standing over Skeeter. You could have heard a pin drop.
Then he just put his hands down over Skeeter's. I
couldn't quite see, but I pictured these normal hands
coming to rest over Skeeter's twitching mitts. We
waited for him to come out of the chair like a comet

and throw the guy out the window. Nobody holds hands with Skeeter.

But something was happening. Skeeter didn't move, and neither did the guy. He was tall enough to have to stoop over Skeeter, but he was pretty thin and no fighter. He wasn't pinning Skeeter's hands there, which wouldn't have been possible. He was just being very calm, and let that calmness flow out of his hands and into Skeeter's. It made no sense, and it worked. Nobody moved, not Ms. Slater, not even Skeeter. Time stopped until the bell rang.

That broke the spell. Skeeter's drooping head jerked up. But he never looked at the other guy. I don't think he understood he was there. Skeeter just slid out of his desk and loped off. Everybody did. At that age, when there's something you can't explain, you walk away from it.

I was in no hurry, though, and neither was Kate Lucas. She was still in her chair, looking back at where Skeeter had been. And so it was just the three of us there. Kate and me and the guy, who was Trav Kirby.

CHAPTER THREE

"So tell me," Kate said to Trav, "how did you work that with Skeeter? I'm interested."

It was lunchtime, and we were in the Slop Shop, which is what we called the cafeteria. I'd happened to be sitting across from Trav at one of the boys' tables. Kate skated up from nowhere and planted herself at the end of the table between us. A girl at a boys' table? Out of the question. All the other guys quickly cleared out.

"By the way, I'm Kate Lucas."

"I'm Trav Kirby."

"This is Buck Mendenhall," Kate said, which amazed me, since I didn't think she even remembered who I was. Things were moving a little too fast for me, as they often do. I didn't know if Trav was going to shake hands with me or not. I wasn't sure how preppie he was.

"I was a hyperactive kid," Trav said, "so I knew the signs."

"You were like Skeeter?" I couldn't believe it. He was too Sub for that, too cool.

"Well, I was a lot younger. But I was bouncing off the walls, and nobody could do anything with me. I was running around flapping my hands, and I couldn't sit still long enough to tie my shoes. I couldn't even watch T.V. without trying to get up and ride the set."

I was impressed, because he really seemed to have everything together now. Both he and Kate seemed older to me, older and knowing things I didn't.

"So what happened?" Kate asked him.

"My parents took me to doctors, so then I was on medication. It only slowed me down. It didn't make changes. They took me to therapists, but they only tried to make me talk when what I really wanted to do was walk on the ceiling."

"But why?" Kate was trying to picture this, to get back there.

"I wonder myself," Trav said. "It started too early to remember. The world just seemed like a big, scary place. I was probably jumpy in the cradle. I guess I thought maybe my parents would just go off and leave me. There's not a lot of logic to that because they're still right there, hanging over me. Boy, are they hanging over me."

He worked his shoulders then, shrugging off his folks, maybe. "I don't know. I just climbed down from it. I think maybe I'm redirecting a lot of that energy or anger or fear or whatever it was. I can still get pretty keyed up over things. I have to watch myself."

He sat back, cool and sure, not a wrinkle in his shirt. I wasn't too certain about what he'd said.

"You think you could cure Skeeter?" Kate was working through an egg salad sandwich. She brought a sack lunch in true Slo fashion. Trav and I had feasted off the school lunch, which is the Sub way. I was eating out of the steam table because I never have time in the mornings to pack a lunch.

"I don't think I could cure anybody," Trav said. "But once in a while you can get somebody through a minute or two."

"You got us all through a minute or two in home-room," Kate said. "Sherrie Slater was running out of luck."

"I know the feeling," Trav said.

The bell rang for fifth period.

"You guys want to come over to my house after school?" Kate said. "We could hang out or whatever."

All the other girls were over at their tables, moni-toring all this with the edges of their eyes. But Kate always made her own rules.

"Watch yourself," I told Trav. "She'll want to show you snake holes."

Kate was on her feet, looking far down upon me with gray eyes. "Snake season is over. They've all wrapped up in big, slimy balls to cuddle all winter down in the ground. Right where you walk. Besides, my snake-hole period was summer before last, when I was just a kid. Things change."

She walked away then, practicing good posture

and maybe wiggling her skinny bottom just a little. And Trav and I followed. For years.

Maybe if we'd all been a little older when we met, Trav and Kate would have paired off and left me hanging. I'll never know, which is just as well. I know there was something special between them, but then, there was something special with the three of us.

For one thing, Kate was a hardcore Slo. Her family had been around here since the earth cooled. Trav was a complete Sub, so they were crossing party lines. Nobody was sure what I was, including me. Worse yet, Kate was a girl and we were guys. So I guess we were reasonably weird.

I don't remember things as they happened. Puberty scrambles your brains. I do remember the time I brought them home to show Trav the mobile home. He didn't seem to grasp the concept of trailer living, so Kate told me to give another tour. I personally think she wanted another look at the place herself.

I showed them around after school one day, and since Dad was still at work, they saw into his bedroom too. Trav was interested. He kept starting to say things.

"You mean you both . . . ? How can you . . . ?"

But then he'd get quiet, not wanting to hurt my feelings. It didn't bother me. I knew we lived pretty different.

Kate ran her finger over some surface. "Don't you guys ever dust this place?"

No, we never do, but Trav looked really disturbed, like she'd made a bad blunder. Gradually, under our influence, he began to take the ways Kate and I lived more for granted. He lightened up a little, at least when we were all together. Not much, but some.

Mainly, we hung out at Kate's. She had to look after her great-grandmother, Polly Prior. Neighbors, including Irene, looked in on Polly during the day, and she was pretty swift with the wheelchair, but she counted on Kate. Kate's mom had a job as a secretary and went out a lot at night, so Kate was actually in charge, which was a key to her.

We hung out together. Maybe not every day. For one thing, Trav turned out to be quite a student, which kept his nose to the grindstone. He was the only kid I knew who really studied in junior high. But it seems now that we were never apart.

I can see now that Trav wouldn't really have fitted in with the other Subs, though he seemed pure Sub to us. He wasn't a big talker, but he liked to talk about things you wouldn't expect. For one thing, he read newspapers. I mean, he could talk to you about the national deficit and Central America. If you gave me all day, I could maybe find Central America on the map.

"The situation's deteriorating," he'd say, about everything. In a way it was funny. This well-groomed, quiet kid in his sharp Members Only Windbreaker and Docksides, talking very seriously about deteriorating situations.

"What's deteriorating?" Polly asked. She was always there, listening.

"Take Latin America," Trav said, ready with his facts. "When Mexico goes, we've got a two-thousand-mile border with them that we won't be able to defend. We can't defend it now."

"How's Mexico going to go?" Polly said. She'd get interested. I think she read the newspaper too. I know she watched Dan Rather on her black-and-white set and talked back to him.

"Revolution," Trav said. "It'll be styled as a popular uprising against corrupt government, and we'll play hands off. Actually, it'll be orchestrated from Moscow, with Cuba doing the actual training and dirty work. It'll be all over while we debate it in Congress."

Polly'd listen, working her chin in her hand, gazing away and then catching glimpses of Trav.

"Take Japan," he'd say. "They're covered by our military umbrella and burying us economically."

He had a lot of examples. And in Trav's mind, countries were always falling and trouble was moving up on us. Kate listened, and the little worry lines formed between her eyebrows.

"Trav," she said once, "don't get so carried away. What can you do about the world, anyway?"

He had gotten pretty carried away. He looked over at her, and his eyes were snapping. "Nothing. That's the point. It's not much fun knowing these things when everybody else is going around with blinders on. You people—"

"Trav, don't." Kate was patient, calm, with him, like he'd been with Skeeter. "When you're grown up, you can do something. You can go into politics or the Army or law or something."

"Be a lawyer like my father?" he said. "Handle divorce cases and overpriced land deals while the world's falling apart? Besides, by the time I'm grown, it'll be too late. It's too late now."

It wasn't always this serious. We wouldn't let it be. We played a lot of games in Polly's kitchen, and Polly rolled herself right up, making a foursome. There's an old oak table in their kitchen, but she always made us put up a card table. It was handier for her wheelchair, and she took her game playing as seriously as Trav took the world situation.

We played some board games, Monopoly mainly, with an ancient set, probably a first edition. Things don't get thrown out at Kate's and Polly's. The Monopoly counters were all cast metal: little 1930's cars and locomotives and top hats. The cards and the play money were all flaking away. We had to make new ones for the Reading Railroad and for both the go-to-jail cards. We had us some real marathon games, leaving the board up for days and getting into major disputes.

Trav played like he lived, building up his supply of houses and hotels, flinching with pain when he landed on somebody else's property, even Baltic Avenue.

"That's not legal," he'd say to Polly about one of her more unorthodox moves or whenever she gave the dice a little extra nudge. "That's completely illegal." She never heard him.

Polly got upset if she couldn't be banker. Trav got upset if he couldn't tie up Boardwalk and Park Place. Kate got upset if Trav was upset. I upset the board once, purely by accident, and everybody got upset. We had some great times.

But Polly got tired of Monopoly. "I was tired of it in 1939," she said. And the oftener she lost, the tireder she got. "This is kid stuff," she'd mumble. "You three got to remember I'm an old woman." So she taught us some card games, "real games," in her opinion: crazy eights, spit in the ocean, all played by her rules. Polly was a demon at cards, playing for blood and sneaking peeks at our hands. She was about bald, and the ceiling light gleamed on the dome of her scalp. All she lacked was a green eyeshade.

"I've outlived everybody I ever knew," she said, "so I'm starting over with you three. When you're all grown up, you can send me your kids. I'm too mean to die." Then she'd flash the ace of spades, which I'd been sure was in Trav's hand.

I guess the little world we had going for ourselves was pretty novel to him. His eyes would travel around the kitchen sometimes. Polly collected calendars, the big ones from implement dealers and banks, and they never got taken down. The kitchen was wallpapered with them, all the way back to the fifties. And there were cut-down Clorox bottles hanging in the windows with ivy growing down from them. Pretty corny, and Trav studied it all, and us.

He could never quite believe I could drive my dad's truck. I was still three years or so away from legal licensing age, but I'd been driving that truck forever, just on back roads with Dad beside me. And Kate—she was in charge around her house. Anything that got done, she did it.

My mom wasn't around, and Kate's dad never had been. And who but Kate had a living great-grandmother, especially one who could shuffle one-handed and cheated at cards? You could tell this was all pretty unusual to Trav. I guess he thought of himself as our resident alien, but he liked our world better. We were all different, but we fitted.

Those afternoons always seemed to end the same way. It'd be getting on for evening, and we'd be playing for blood. The winners didn't want to quit, and the losers wanted to catch up. But then Trav would check his watch, like a busy executive.

"Got to break this up," he'd say, looking around for his books and his calculator. "If I don't get home, my parents will kill me."

I figured his family had him pretty programmed. But I guess Polly thought otherwise. She seemed to think he was programming himself.

She looked up at him one time, pretty sharp. It was crazy eights, and she must have been winning. "What'll they use?" she asked him.

We all looked up. Polly could come out with some strange sayings once in a while.

"I say, what'll your folks use to kill you with? Shot-

gun? Hunting knife? Weed-n-Feed in your oatmeal?
They sound like mighty desperate characters to me."

Trav was edging his chair back. He gave Polly half
a crooked grin. "I don't think I want to find out," he
said, "so I better be getting home."

He kept a schedule, and when he decided it was
time to go, he went.

After he'd gone one time, Kate said, "Trav's wound
up too tight. He's in too big a hurry to grow up."

Polly was collecting the cards to lay out a hand of
solitaire. "He ain't in a hurry to grow up," she said.
"He dreads it."

We had each other and it helped. I was beginning
to develop, at least physically, but nothing seemed to
be the right size. Every morning I woke up, I had to
check me out to see who was there. Some mornings I
was a kid. Some mornings I was a maniac. Some
mornings I didn't wake up at all: I just sleepwalked
through the day.

I could have cared less about school once I figured
out the teachers didn't have horns, but Trav slugged
it. The thanks he got was that they kicked him up
into all the gifted classes: computer math and advanced English and super science. I was happy
where I was, but Trav was pushing himself.

Kate took her own path. Schoolwork, lots of things,
seemed to come easy for her, but she had responsibilities at home. Even though she studied, she kept
herself out of the fast-track classes. She was always
sprinting along about a mile ahead of Trav and me. If

Kate was any example, puberty for girls looked like a piece of cake.

Occasionally she'd come up with a somewhat naive notion. One thing pretty obvious was that Trav wasn't as easy around his family as he was with us. I guess at that age, anybody with a home never wants to go home to it. But again Trav seemed to take things to extremes. Personally, I was pretty glad to see Dad when he got off work, especially when he was working long hours on overtime. And Kate was at home a lot, because she had responsibilities. But things seemed to be different at Trav's house. I wondered if maybe things worked so smooth in the Sub way at the Kirbys' that Trav didn't have much role to play around home. It made Kate and me a little curious about the Kirbys. I guess the Kirbys were a little curious about us too.

"Guess what I got," Kate said one day. It was around Christmas.

We were playing cards, and all Polly said was "Don't dawdle and discard."

But Kate put her cards down, reached into the pocket of her tomboy jeans, and pulled up a crumpled envelope addressed to Miss Kate Lucas. It was high-quality paper, and so was the card inside. Trav took one look at it, groaned, and threw his hand in.

"Read it out loud," Polly said. Her vision was at its best when she was staring at face cards or a run of anything in a single suit.

With a sideways glance at Trav, Kate began to read: " 'Ellen and Mitch Kirby request the pleasure of your company at a holiday housewarming for their new home, Eighteen Loire Drive, Greenbriar, on the Saturday before Christmas. Buffet at eight.' "

This part was printed or maybe engraved with holly leaves—very nice work. There was more added in Mrs. Kirby's handwriting across the bottom: " 'Do come, Kate, and bring your parents. We're looking forward to meeting you.' "

Trav's fist hit the table, vibrating Polly. "I told them you don't have—both parents, Kate. They never hear anything I say. Why did I even tell them I know you?"

"Did you tell them you know me?" I said pretty quick.

Somehow the idea of getting an invitation like this from grown-ups struck me as a little eerie. Like a summons, or a report card mailed directly to your home. Trav nodded.

"They want to know where I am, so I tell them what I need to tell them. You don't have to come, Kate. You either, Buck. Forget it."

"Well, that ain't too nice a way to look at it," Polly said. She'd given up any hope for the game. "It could be your party, too, and your friends."

"You don't understand, Polly." All Trav's cool was gone. "My mother's been planning this party for six months, ever since we moved in. It's going to be perfect. Too perfect."

Polly took this in behind her moon glasses. Kate was thinking it over, too, and coming up with a Kate-type idea.

"Look, Trav," she said, "we know you haven't particularly wanted us to hang around your house."

"You think I'm ashamed of you or something? Because I'm not."

"No," Kate said, very wise, "it's just that this party could break the ice. Why make a major thing out of it? I'd like to come. Besides, I have a dynamite idea."

We were in trouble right there.

"My mother can come, and Buck's dad can bring her."

"Hoo-boy," said Polly Prior.

"Wait a minute, Kate," I said, "I'm not too sure—"

"Why not?" Kate said.

I couldn't quite put my finger on why not. You'd just catch glimpses of Kate's mom. She zipped in and out. I think she knew quite a few men, too, without adding Dad. Once when she was going out, Kate called out after her, "I want you home by midnight, Mother. And alone."

"I think it could be interesting," Kate said. She was revving up already.

"Hoo-boy," said Polly.

I figured Dad would just say no. When it came to social life, he hadn't gone farther than Irene and Scotty's back stairs. It wouldn't have dawned on me that adults can get lonely too.

But I showed him my invitation with the same message about inviting my parents too. He examined it and stood there, flicking the stiff cardboard with a big, bruised-black fingernail.

"Do you want me to go?" he said.

"Well . . ." Then I told him about Kate's plan.

At that point I thought he'd definately bow out, but he just looked surprised. He gets these little lines fanning out from his eyes when he's thinking over something.

"What's her mother like?" he said.

"Dad, you're on your own there."

CHAPTER FOUR

That party must have been the first time I ever wore a tie. It was one of Dad's and lapped way down over my fly. I didn't own a suit, but I had a sport coat, and I got a pair of leather penny loafers for the occasion, unsneakering my feet.

You could walk to the Kirbys' house from Kate's place, even though it was in quite a different world. She and I started out on foot. We were about the last people in the entire area who walked anyplace. Somehow I couldn't picture the two of us riding in the open bed of Dad's GMC truck with him and her mom up front in the cab. Besides, Kate's mom was still getting dressed.

"And dressed and dressed and dressed," said Kate.

It was a great night with a moon, frosty and no mud. Kate had on a party dress and what looked like pantyhose. I wasn't much into clothes then, mine or anybody else's. She had on new shoes, too, not heels but dress-up. She walked different in them, more graceful. Every once in a while I happened to notice

Kate was a girl. Every time I noticed, I was more impressed, but I didn't want her to change too much. I didn't want any of us to change.

The suburb of Greenbriar was filling in on two sides of us. It hadn't eaten up the horse farm, but it was heading that way. Construction was easing off for the winter, but there'd been a lot of housing starts through the fall, and whole neighborhoods were rising out of the ground. Unfinished framework showed up against the moon.

"It'll all be built up one day," Kate said softly. "All new houses and streets and people, like any place else. We'll remember when it was still a little corner of the country. We'll be like Polly, remembering things she doesn't even tell because they don't matter to anybody else."

That would have been a good time to take her hand as we walked along. But I didn't know how, and maybe I didn't need to.

Greenbriar broke down into distinct categories. At the top of the line and a small rise of land, Loire Drive swept up in an easy curve, newly paved. The sod on the lawns hadn't taken root yet. No sidewalks, of course. These people had wheels: Mercedes-Benz, Ferrari, Jag-U-ar. Trav had pointed out his mother once, barreling along on the crown of the road in a Peugeot wagon loaded with options. His dad drove a BMW.

Loire Drive was a cul-de-sac, which is Greenbriar talk for a dead-end road. At the end was the Kirbys' house. It was French style, I guess: slate roof, rosy pink used brick, big double white doors between carriage lamps. There were oversize Christmas wreaths around the carriage lamps, and a lot of cars in the drive already. I tried to picture Dad's rust-orange truck pulling in there.

Mr. Kirby opened the doors to us. I don't know what I was expecting: a big loud guy, I guess, in a Christmas-colored vest and a big red face to go with it. He wasn't like that at all. He was wearing a dark suit, and he had some gray in his hair: nice-looking, thin-faced. In fact, he was a Trav except about thirty years older.

"You're Kate and Buck," he said, not loud, and put out his hand so I knew we were going to shake. He eased Kate's coat off, pretty much in the same gesture. You could see the living room was full of grown-ups. Some of the women had on long dresses, and there was only a quiet murmur of voices and a tinkle of drinks.

"Don't mind them," Mr. Kirby said. "We're glad Trav's got company too." He didn't even call him Travis, which is Trav's real name.

Mrs. Kirby appeared then, detaching herself from the living room. She was a quiet-type lady with blondish hair, and she was wearing a long dress. I didn't personally think she made too big of an impression, but I noticed Kate noticing her.

Somehow Mrs. Kirby drew us a little farther into the entrance hall. Then there was this guy standing at the foot of the stairs. He reached out for the stair

railing, but it was wrapped around with prickly ever-
green, so he drew his hand back.

He was wearing a wine-colored blazer and dark
pants, spit-shined shoes. He had on a silk tie tied tight
over a gold collar pin. I didn't quite know him at first.
It was Trav.

He was poised there on the bottom step, and I
thought he'd just tell us to come on up to his room
and get away from the perfect party. The concept of
having your own room with your own door on it
intrigued me somewhat.

But he stepped up and put out his hand, just like
his dad. We shook hands. I guess it was etiquette, but
I wondered who we were supposed to be that evening. Kate, of course, was taking everything in.

I thought his folks would loom over us, but they
just melted back into the party. Kate took Trav's arm,
and we went into the big living room together. You
had the feeling Kate wanted to say what a spectacu-
lar place it was and how neat all the decorations
were, but something in Trav held her back.

At the end of the room was a table set up with
punch and food. I thought that was the buffet table,
but it wasn't.

Trav wasn't saying much, but what impressed me
was how he was like his parents. I saw where he'd
learned to be a perfectionist. He worked just as hard
on his schoolwork as his mother had worked on this
party. He was part of us, but he was part of them too.

"Face it, Trav," Kate said finally. "This is a great
party in a beautiful house."

Trav shrugged, and then he grinned. He didn't do that a lot. When he did, it really lit up his somewhat severe face. "It's okay," he said.

People, grown people, kept arriving, enlarging the party, and were introduced around. Kate was having a fine time, swilling punch and wolfing down little finger-shaped sandwiches. "What we have here," she said, "is high Sub culture."

"We have definitely hit the major league," I said, but low so Trav wouldn't hear.

Then we were all treated to an unusual sight. Standing in the doorway from the hall were this man and this woman, my dad and Kate's mom. I was more used to seeing Dad in a hardhat, but he had on his suit, the blue one, and he was wearing the other tie. His neck looked a little tight in his collar, and he'd wet-combed his hair. He has a good head of hair, even around back, and his shoulders were extra big in the suit coat.

Here's something I noticed. Every woman in the room turned for a look at him. I hadn't exactly seen my own dad as super-stud before, but he was beginning to show tendencies.

I guess everybody noticed Kate's mom beside him, hanging on his arm. I'd seen her before, but now I really saw her. Her hair was teased way up over her head, and it was blond of a completely different order from Mrs. Kirby's. I'm talking blinding blond. There wasn't much to the top part of her dress except fringe, and she had on a major amount of jewelry. She looked a little like Loretta Lynn in Dolly

Parton's dress. She peered into the room with a big red smile fixed on her lips.

"Hoo-boy," said Kate.

Then, being Kate, she just sighed a little and started across the room, bringing Trav and me with her. Anybody else but Kate would have gone the other way—out the French window, possibly.

"Now, let me get this straight," Mrs. Kirby was saying. "You're Kate's mother, and you're Buck's father. Is that right?"

"Shoot, call me Janis," Kate's mom said, loud enough for the whole room. "What a house! I'd hate to have to clean it."

"She'd hate to have to clean ours," Kate muttered out of the side of her mouth, and then remembered to smile.

"Just time for a drink before dinner," Mr. Kirby said.

"Make mine a—"

"Hello, Mother," Kate said, stepping up.

Kate's mom peered at her. "Oh! Kate, it's you!" Her bracelets jangling, she grabbed Kate and wedged her right into her bust. People really noticed. "This is my baby girl," she said to Mrs. Kirby. "Why, I had her when I was a teenager myself, so we're more like sisters than anything else."

Everybody in the room heard that. I don't know who believed it. Kate just stood there, very still.

Other doors opened then, and there was this dining room and a huge table with candles and many mounds of food, all gourmet. It was a very fine scene.

"Does that chandelier remind you of something?" Kate said out of the corner of her mouth.

"No," I said. "What?"

"One of Mother's earrings."

We joined the line around the table, and Trav helped Kate load her plate, being a good host. It was a real feast. You could hear Kate's mom laughing uproariously at anything Dad might be saying.

After dinner, people gravitated into groups of people they already knew, somewhat like teenagers. Dad happened to mention to Mr. Kirby that he'd helped build this house, and that got Mr. Kirby interested. Since he's a lawyer, he didn't know much about construction and had a lot of questions. This drew in some of the other men, and Dad became a sort of center of attention.

But the other women didn't draw in Kate's mom. She hung in there by Dad, pretending she was interested in joists and copper piping and dry wall. Kate and Trav and I were hanging out around the Christmas tree, a mammoth blue spruce with all-white lights.

Mrs. Kirby sort of magically appeared beside Trav. "Perhaps you'd like to give Kate's mother a tour of the house," she said. "She's rather at a loose end."

So Trav rounded up Kate's mom, whose eyes were beginning to glaze over. We started off through the house: Mr. Kirby's study with all his lawbooks on shelves, the family room, the powder room, the kitchen, the front hall, the back hall. Kate's mom gushed over all of it.

"This is one fantastic layout," she kept saying. "This is what I call living high on the hog."

She took Trav by the arm, like he was Dad, and wanted to see everything. Kate and I followed along.

When we finished with the downstairs, we went upstairs through all six bedrooms, ending with Trav's.

I don't know what I expected. A complete sound system, I suppose, a room-size TV screen, computer terminals popping out of the walls, though I'm not sure why. I expected a lot of stuff plus plenty of interior decoration, and I was wrong.

It was all new, of course, just moved into. And Trav had his desk all set up with his books and things for a science project and a Canon portable electric typewriter, a Typestar 5.

But the rest of the room was younger than Trav. He'd brought along with him a lot of things he'd had as a younger kid, quite a lot younger. Collections and toys. I don't mean he was still playing with them. They were all arranged very neat on shelves above the books, as neat and orderly as the rest of the house. There were over a hundred Matchbox toy cars, jars of marbles, baseball cards, games still in their original boxes, a few Ninja items, some wooden educational toys that must have gone way back. It seemed funny to me—more than that.

Trav didn't seem to be embarrassed by them. "I had one of those," Kate said, because he even had a stuffed toy there, a Paddington Bear. It was propped way over in a corner, but it was there.

Trav saw me being surprised at this little nest from the past. He shrugged.

"They tear up your roots. They get more and more successful, and they just expect you to walk away from everything. You have to move on to a new place, a bigger house. You want something that's yours, so you can remember yourself."

He jerked at his necktie hard, and the little gold tie pin popped loose.

We stood there, and even Kate's mom was quiet, watching him. Then Kate said, "That makes me think of Polly."

That really surprised her mom. "What are you talking about, Kate? Nobody ever uprooted her. Who could? She's lived in that same old house forever."

"I know," Kate said. "She was lucky."

I walked her home after the party. I remember the little outdoor Christmas lights on the new shrubs of the Greenbriar lawns and how the Kirbys' house glowed behind us up on the rise. I remember how Kate seemed a little tired, dragging along in her new shoes.

"I have really got to deal with myself," she said. The cold made little plumes in front of her mouth.

"What about?"

"About my mother. I'm ashamed of her, and it's really immature. I've got to get over that. I've really got to work on that."

"Well, your mom's got a lot of . . . personality," I said, which I thought sounded safe.

"She's just who she is," Kate said. "I know that. Why can't I deal with it?"

I was interested because Kate never seemed to let herself get down. She wasn't big on confessing to weaknesses, either.

"You're not worried that you're going to grow up like her, are you?"

Kate shook her head. "She never really grew up herself. Polly and I raised me. You can see that. And Mother was really intimidated by that party, which didn't help. But did you notice how nice the Kirbys were to her? Some of their friends may be snobs, but they aren't. They could have frozen her out, but they didn't."

I guess I'd noticed that.

"Sometimes I can get annoyed with Trav," she said. "He really resents his parents, which doesn't make a lot of sense. And you know why he resents them."

"I do?"

"Because he's exactly like them."

"Then why—"

"Why not?" Kate said. "When you're as uncomfortable with yourself as Trav is and you see the very same traits in your parents, then you just turn on them. You want to shift the blame onto them and get out from under it yourself. But it's immature. Besides, boys—"

"Hold it," I said. "Let's not hear that stuff about boys being more immature than girls or whatever. You just said yourself you're immature."

Kate paced along. "There are different levels of immaturity," she said, muttering somewhat.

I paced along by her side, and I have to admit, I wasn't too unhappy to hear her finding a small flaw in Trav. I was already a little worried that the two of them might drift off together, leaving me out.

"Parents." Kate shook her head. "You're lucky, Buck. You're not hung up about your dad." She sighed a small sigh. "Besides, he's a real hunk."

That brought me back down to earth.

Then, when we got back to Kate's place, there was Polly. When she didn't have anyplace else to be, she always sat with her chair rolled up to the kitchen stove. It didn't throw off any heat, being electric. But I guess she remembered other times when people sat around a kitchen range.

She'd been dozing and wouldn't admit it, though she looked around somewhat dazed. Kate went straight over and turned the heat on under the kettle.

"How about a little cup of tea, Polly?" The cold air had put roses in Kate's cheeks, and Polly put up her old crooked hand and brushed Kate's face.

Then Kate plunged her hands down into her coat pocket. "What have we here? Good grief, the canapé bandit has struck again!"

And she pulls up all kinds of stuff: little finger sandwiches, Christmas cookies, fancy crackers, all kinds of portable eats swiped off the Kirbys' refreshment table and all wrapped in Christmas napkins. How she worked that I will never know. And old Polly's watching it pile up.

"I'd have brought you some dips," Kate said, "but they'd have turned my pockets into churning swamps."

"There's a deviled egg," Polly said. "I like them."

Kate put all these borrowed goodies onto a plate and picked off the pocket lint.

"This is how Mrs. Kirby serves everything," she said, "very attractively arranged."

Then she poured out water over a teabag, and Polly wheeled up to the kitchen table and had herself a party too. Kate had been thinking about bringing some of the party to Polly. She'd been planning that all evening.

"How'd your mother behave?" Polly inquired.

"Just eat, Polly," Kate said. "Don't ask."

I waited up late for Dad that night, which was a new experience. I waited up partly because I couldn't get my necktie off without ripping it to shreds. Before Dad got home, I about burned out the old Sony watching late movies, which were changing over to Sunday Sunrise Sermonettes before I heard the truck.

The trailer door opened, letting in a blast of winter night and Dad.

"That woman's a dancin' fool," he was saying as he climbed in. "I'm bushed."

I was sprawled out on the Hide-A-Bed, and his head was up there by the ceiling. Dancing?

"She wanted to go down the route to Billy's Bluegrass, where they all know her," Dad said. "I feel like I been rode hard and put up wet."

He sat down in the chair and jerked his shoes off and looked at his feet. "They're swelling. I haven't danced since . . . I don't know when."

He puffed up his cheeks and blew out the air. "I must be getting old. Come on over here. I'll get that tie off you." His was already pulled loose.

While I was bending over him, I said, "Kate's not much like her mom." I guess that was obvious, but I mentioned it.

"Her mom's something else," Dad said. "She was easier in her mind when we got down to Billy's. All she needed was some loud music and a smoky room and a bunch of good old country boys stomping up a storm. The Kirbys just weren't her style."

He sat there, grinning back at the evening. He didn't look totally bushed.

"I like the Kirbys," he said. "They aren't my style either, but they're fine people. They make you welcome."

I thought about that, how Dad could meet any kind of people, and he liked them and they liked him. I saw that was who I wanted to be—somebody like him. I hadn't known till then.

"You going to take Kate's mom out again?" I had to ask. I was really curious.

"Janis? No way. I'm not ready for some things. And some things I'll never be ready for." He waited a moment and then said, "Got that?"

It seemed clear enough. I'd shut off the Sony, and you could hear the wind around the trailer. I thought Dad was going to nod off right there in the chair, but he was more awake than he looked.

"I'm glad you've got friends here," he said, easing into something. "I worried about that. Oh, I don't mean I worried. I just had it in mind. I didn't know if you'd be satisfied here . . . just the two of us."

The wind whined around the trailer, looking for a way in.

"Do you think we're making it all right, Bucky?"

I never have been able to break Dad of calling me Bucky. And I didn't know what to say to him.

"The two of us here, rattling around in this old tin can," he said. "I don't know. I had all kinds of big plans, and they're still right there out of reach, where they always were. I can't give you everything other people give their sons."

I really didn't want to hear that. Dad and I didn't get into that type conversation.

"I can't be everything I'd like to be, for either one of us. I can't even give you what a lot of people would call a real home. But I would if I could. I'd give you the moon if I could get it down."

It was quiet then. Dad, bulked big in the chair, was looking off to one side, squinting into a distance that wasn't there. The rest of the world was asleep, I guess. Across the orchard, Kate in her room. Trav, up the hill, in his room surrounded by his old toys.

My hands just kept picking at loose threads in the Hide-A-Bed.

"I don't need it, Dad," I told him. "I don't need the moon."

CHAPTER FIVE

Some things are just meant to be, and I ought to have seen one of them coming. Skeeter Calhoun and I were going to tangle.

Skeet had spent a busy winter doing serious structural damage to the school and terrorizing teachers. The only good thing about him was you didn't see him on a regular basis if you were still alive after homeroom every morning. He was in all the slow classes, and he wasn't too steady about school attendance, which nobody minded. He roamed around a lot. You'd see him sometimes, in the distance if you were lucky, trudging along a road or coming across an open field like he'd just dropped down out of a tree.

But one day along toward spring Kate came up to me in the hall. Nodding over her shoulder, she said, "Am I seeing things, or what?"

I looked off down the hall, and there was old Skeet. He was hanging out beside the drinking fountain under the Commitment to Quality Education plaque. Nobody seemed to be thirsty that day. He had on his year-long overalls and a sweat shirt. It looked like the sleeves of it had been bitten off by wild beasts. But what I particularly noticed was the hardhat on his head. It was a bright orange construction worker's hardhat. It was Dad's.

The thing is, Dad had a habit of leaving his hardhat outside the trailer when he came home at night. He left it on the bumper of the truck, on the front step, anywhere around, and then he grabbed it up the next morning on the way to work. We have enough loose stuff rolling around inside the trailer without that. Dad had an extra one too in the truck, but this particular orange one was his Number One hardhat. It had MENDENHALL stenciled right across the front of it. So when I saw it crammed down on Skeeter Calhoun's Neanderthal brow, there was not too much question in my mind.

I had this clear picture of how he must have wandered past our place, spotted the hardhat, barely managed to read the name Mendenhall on it, and figured it was the ideal souvenir. It will not pull a muscle in your brain to follow Skeeter's thought patterns.

I strolled past him. He was working his hands together, popping his knuckles. His biceps were bulging under the raggedy remnants of his sleeves. Under the rigid brim of the hardhat he saw me see him. I strolled on, deep in thought.

I'd been meaning to work out all winter. I wasn't shooting up in height like Trav, but I was filling out.

I'd been meaning to pump a little iron but hadn't gotten around to it. And now this.

"I've got to get that hardhat back," I mentioned to Kate and Trav between sixth and seventh period. We just happened to be there together between classes as we often happened to be.

"Just forget it," Kate said. "It'll only mean trouble."

"Trouble's what Skeeter wants," I said. "Otherwise he wouldn't be flashing around my dad's hardhat. It's got my dad's name on it, for Pete's sake—*my* name. Everybody can see that. You better believe Skeeter wants trouble."

"Do you?" said Kate.

"I want that hat back."

"Let me talk to him," Trav said. He took hold of my arm, but he didn't look confident. He looked a little white around the lips.

"Words won't work," I said. "Skeeter's way past that. He's getting out of control."

"So let him," Trav said. "We'll stick together and keep out of his way. He doesn't have that much of an attention span."

"You people don't understand," I said, warming up under the collar. "I don't want him to forget. I want that hat back. Just let me alone and I'll take care of it."

Brave words. The bell rang.

"I hate violence," Kate said, moving off. She gave me a flinty backward glance with her cool gray eyes.

What she really meant was she didn't want to see me reduced to an inanimate object.

Somehow I got through that last period of the day. I had the impression that it could be my last period. Period. Then, when school was over, I cut out quick, needing to avoid Kate and Trav in case they had a plan for saving my skin and extending my productive years.

But I couldn't find Skeeter. Okay, I didn't look under every rock, but I checked out the general environment of the school. Here I was, willing to sacrifice my life for a good cause, and I couldn't find Skeeter. Then it dawned on me he probably hadn't even gone to seventh period. What did Skeeter need with a full school day?

I started home. At least I still had my health. I figured that after a sleepless night I'd tackle him early the next morning. Maybe I could take him on down by the gym, and the coach might come along and separate us. And save me.

I was almost home, going past Polly's pear orchard. I saw a glint of something orange in among the branches, and then Skeeter stepped out of the trees. Just the two of us. Just like he'd planned.

"Mendenhall," he said. The hardhat was down to his snoutlike nose. His big hands were on his hips. It seemed to me he'd put on some weight, especially around the shoulders. I froze in the road. There was a deep ditch between us, and he was up high on the far side.

"Let's have the hat, Skeeter."

I could hear him breathing.

"Come and get it, wussy."

I started to. I walked over to the side of the road, then down into the ditch, which made no sense at all because he was right up there above me on a small cliff. I was down in the ditch, staring into the toes of his boots.

"So come on down," I said. "Let's fight it out and get it over with."

He was looking down at me, his glittering pig eyes shaded by the brim of my dad's hardhat. I guess the concept of a fair fight confused him, even though he was bound to win it. He seemed to expect me to beg for the hat, or maybe for mercy.

Somehow that really made me mad. Without giving it much thought, I lunged out, grabbed both his ankles, and pulled his feet out from under him. Like in a cartoon, the hardhat shot right off as his head jerked back. I heard the hat light with a hollow thunk behind him in the trees as he crashed down on me like a house. His rump grazed the overhang, but I took his full weight. We ended up in the bottom of the ditch. I was pretty sure he'd broken every bone in my body without even making a fist.

When he got his breath back, he seemed to like things the way they were, with him on top. He worked around until he was sitting on my chest. He weighed a ton. Still, I'd brought him down, and that bothered him.

He had me at a slight disadvantage. I could breathe out, though not in. But my hands were free. I was spread-eagled in the wet ditch, but my hands were still attached to my arms. We both realized this at the same moment. He shifted around and brought both his bootheels down on both my hands. Metal cleats cut little hot half-moons into my palms.

"You want your daddy's hat back," Skeeter grunted, "you got to pay for it."

He couldn't get much leverage, sitting down on me as he was, but he hauled off and his fist landed on my glass jaw. Every one of my teeth moved, separately. I took the next blow in the left temple. And some more. I really saw red, and it was my blood. Finally it all seemed to be happening to somebody else, and off I drifted, someplace past pain.

I thought it was my heart beating, but then it seemed to be the sound of running feet. Far off, possibly in a tunnel. My eyelids seemed to be enlarging, but I could open them. Blue sky. Could be anywhere. Could even be—

I sat bolt upright, in a ditch, my face and hands on fire. Then there they were, these two heads. Trav's and Kate's. They were red-faced, panting. Kate was dragging a strand of hair away from her mouth. Trav was snow white around the lips. I knew them quite well. They were friends of mine, and any minute now I'd remember why I was in a wet ditch.

"Where were you?" Kate barked. "Why did you let this happen?"

She was stamping around in the dirt, hopping mad, apparently at me. Then she got a good view of my face.

"Oh, no. I can't stand this. Look at you."

She was practically jumping up and down now, and her hands were over her face. She was carrying on in a very un-Kately way. "We looked all over for you, and you didn't have any more sense than to—"

"Kate," Trav said, "shut up."

She did, quick. They went to work getting me out of the ditch. Trav reached down and took both my hands. The pressure on my chewed-up palms really hurt, and I stumbled up on my feet so he'd turn me loose. When he did, he saw his hands were messed with my blood. His face turned an ashy color, and he made the mistake of wiping his hands on his Windbreaker.

I tested my jaw. It hurt bad but worked. All my teeth had settled back into my gums, but one tooth had gouged out part of my lip. I was bleeding down my front.

"Come on," Kate said. "Let's get him to my house. We've got to get some antiseptic or something."

My hands were hanging down, and little trickles of blood were running off my fingers. Kate's eyes closed momentarily.

"I don't think that's such a good idea," Trav said. "I don't think Polly should see this."

"Polly?" Kate said. "What about Buck? Polly can take it."

"Let's not upset her," Trav said, reasonable, gentle.

"Then *what*?"

"Irene." My head was clearing, and I thought of

Irene for some reason, so that's where we went, down the road toward Scotty's Sunoco. Then I threw on my brakes.

"The hardhat. I gotta get it."

"Will you *forget* that thing?" Kate said very loud in my ear. "You're *obsessed.*"

"Where is it?" Trav said.

"Back up there." I jerked my head over my shoulder and experienced an all-new rush of pain. "If he left it, you can't miss it."

Trav swerved up back by the trees, looking for it while Kate entertained me. "You could bleed to death here in the road while Trav pokes around for that thing. I hope you know you're as dumb and crazy as Skeeter."

I just stood there and tried to bleed with dignity.

Trav leaped back over the ditch, swinging Dad's hat by the strap. He dangled it before me so I couldn't miss it, and we went off down the road, me in the middle.

"Wear it," I said to him.

"The hat? Why?"

"I want to see it on a friendly head."

So he humored me and put it on. This, too, seemed to tick Kate off. "I do not understand male psychology." She kicked some gravel. "It does not make any sense."

Irene was out in her garden, raking up brush and trying to rush the season. She was scarecrow tall out there in the rows, her long elbows flying.

Irene was a private kind of person, and not much

showed in her face. She could play poker with Polly and win. Still, the first sight of me shook her. The way people were reacting to my new Skeeterized face was beginning to hurt my feelings.

She sent us all up her back stairs, which I personally found quite a climb. Scotty and Irene's apartment over the Sunoco was mainly one room, and long-armed Irene could reach all over it. She went to work on me with the alcohol and the witch hazel and the gauze and the clean rags. Some of it soothed, some of it stung, but I was in good hands.

Most of my wounds were on the surface, and once in a while Irene would step back and eye her handiwork. Finally, she wadded up the gory T-shirt she'd skinned off me and tossed it behind her into the trash.

"All right, how'd this happen?" Irene was a woman of very few words.

"A roadgrader got me," I explained through a split lip. "Big yellow one with steel treads."

Kate said, "He was so dumb that he—"

"Fight," Trav said.

He'd stood right with me while Irene patched me up, and I could see everything by watching him. He was like a mirror. He didn't flinch when I did, but what was happening to me was happening to him. The only difference was that while my eyes were swelling, his were filling with tears. I didn't want that to be happening. He was taking this harder than I was, which was typical of him. He was feeling too much, as usual, and he was as skinned and raw inside as I was on the outside. Then Irene got between us, and that helped.

She got the whole story out of us, which made me feel like a fool. Even then I was beginning to think this entire thing could have been avoided, though I wasn't admitting it.

Irene looked back and forth at us. She observed Dad's hat, which was like a huge, high-tech mushroom on Trav's narrow head. Since Irene and Scotty had no kids of their own, she didn't have too much idea of the type stuff we get into. I sat slumped on the stool while things like pullet eggs formed all over my face.

Then Kate said, "Something's got to be done about Skeeter."

"Forget the school administration," I said through my new lips. "They'll look the other way. If they were going to deal with Skeeter, they'd have done it. He's given them plenty of reason."

"I'm not talking about school," Kate said.

"Legally," Trav said, "there's—"

"I'm not talking about the law," Kate said. She had our full attention now, Irene's too.

"I'll get Skeeter," Kate said. "I don't know how, but I'll find a way. It may take me a while, but I'll get him."

Irene looked down at Kate, and you could see she was impressed. But I was thinking: That's all I need, a girl fighting my battles. I was willing for us all to go out of the battle business right now.

Then Dad's truck pulled up outside. It was getting

on for evening, and he was home from work. Irene heard his truck door slam, and then she did a surprising thing, very quick.

She reached over to Trav and whipped the hardhat off his head. In three long strides she was out on the landing at the top of the stairs. We could see her out there through the screen door, the hardhat in her hand.

"Mendenhall!" she yelled down at Dad. "Heads up!" I'd never heard her raise her voice before. "Keep this fool thing inside your trailer from now on!"

Then she wound up, hauled off, and threw the hardhat overhand in a magnificent forward pass. We could see it, orange and descending like the sun.

Dad must have caught it. We heard a thunking sound and the wind going out of him.

CHAPTER SIX

I spent that summer in Cleveland, which wasn't exactly the jungle I'd pictured. It was this big city on a reasonably cool lake. Fred Wunderlich went out of his way to make me more or less welcome. We went to a couple of Indian home games, but didn't stretch ourselves out of shape trying to be pals.

It was good to be with Mom, but we were both changed and had to scout around a little to find conversation. She was Mrs. Wunderlich, somewhat citified and shorter than I remembered. They lived in a tidy apartment in a high-rise, sort of like newlyweds, which as a matter of fact they were.

It wasn't a bad summer, but I watched too many reruns, and from the middle of August I was gearing up for home. Mom noticed that, and it hurt her. I ought to have had enough control to keep her from seeing I was about sitting on my duffel bag, waiting to go.

"All we do is say good-bye," she said when she saw me off at the bus station Labor Day morning. I was a head taller than she was by then, but whether that made things easier or not is hard to say.

When Dad took me off the bus at this end, he let me drive the truck home. I was only about four months, three weeks, and a day from my learner's permit anyhow. Dad had his big arm propped out his window, casual.

Then he said, "I thought maybe they'd keep you up in Cleveland. It crossed my mind."

I concentrated on not riding the clutch. "They're doing all right without me."

"Well, that's good," he said. "That's fine."

We were on the truck route south, halfway home. "You get along without me okay?" I said.

"Who, me? Never noticed you were gone."

So I swung around and popped him one with my powerhouse left without even swerving off the road and climbing a guardrail.

When we turned off onto the county road, Scotty's Sunoco was business as usual, but the horse farm was gone. They'd razed the buildings and were grading the land. There was a layer of yellow clay dust over the whole vicinity. A sign was posted in the former pasture:

COMING SOON
TOWN & COUNTRY MALL
28 SELECTED BOUTIQUE–STYLE
SHOPS DESIGNED WITH THE
GREENBRIAR LIFESTYLE IN MIND

Somehow that reminded me of a war, with bulldoz-
ers instead of tanks, and little countries surrendering,
one by one.

"You'll see a few changes, now you're back," Dad
said, which was quite an understatement. I seemed
to have been in a time warp. The past never is where
you left it, and I have a problem with change.

I spent that first evening with Dad and Irene and
Scotty out on their back stairs. We watched it get
dark over our little corner of reality, sippin' and
strummin' and being together. I didn't try to call
Kate or Trav. The phone was too much like long
distance, and I'd had enough of that.

But the next morning early I went looking for
Kate, hoping in a wimpy way that I wouldn't find her
and Trav together.

I found Polly Prior first, out on her back porch with
her chair aimed toward the orchard. She caught a
glimpse of me coming up on her out of the corner of
her lens. I figured she'd missed me a little, but I knew
not to expect a big welcome.

"That orchard ain't worth the powder and shot to
blow it up," she remarked, mainly to herself. That
orchard was her pride and joy, her place. That
orchard stood between her and the world and always
had.

"It don't bear," she said, deciding to recognize me.
"The fruit's not fit to eat, what there is of it. You have
to spray to keep the bugs off. You got to run an
orchard like a business, or you might just as well burn
it down."

I let her talk. It meant something. She could talk like a crazy old lady, but it was an act. "Where you been?" she said. "I haven't had a decent game all summer."

"The game season's about to begin, Polly," I told her. "We're going to have us the world series of Crazy Eights."

She gave me an owlish look.

"Where's Kate?"

"Down there in the orchard where she goes." Polly bent a finger past me into the trees. "She says this is her last day before captivity, meaning school, so she's going to fritter it away. I expect she's got an eye out for you." Polly eyed me herself. "Though she didn't say so."

"Where's Trav?"

"Oh, he's off to foreign parts. I forget which ones. He'll be back for school tomorrow, I reckon." She pulled the purse strings on her mouth extra tight. "They been thick as thieves all summer, them two. You got some catching up to do." She gave me a sly look through both moons.

"You're definitely the meanest old woman in Slocum Township," I told her.

"Number One," she said, bringing up a finger. "You're about growed. Are you shaving yet?"

I bent over and stuck my chin in her face. She reached up and felt it.

"Peach fuzz," said Polly Prior.

A lot of limbs were down in the orchard. I started along the rows, wondering if I was going to have to thrash around all morning to find Kate, wondering what she was doing down here anyway.

Then pretty soon I came to a little clearing where a few trees were missing, a little hideout place I'd never seen before. It couldn't have been far from the back of the trailer, but it felt like miles away. It had an atmosphere, too, lived in, like a room. The unpruned trees were almost walls. The weedy ground was little soft footstools and shaggy carpet.

A girl was there, sitting on a blanket, leaning against the trunk of a fallen pear tree. A girl in shorts and a skimpy stretch top that left her shoulders bare and brown. Her legs were brown, too, long and sensational. A pair of poems crossed at the ankles.

Kate, of course: three months later. She was reading a book and running her hand back through her hair. I don't like change, but I had to admit it. She was turning beautiful on me, so beautiful it made my eyes sting.

"Want to see a foal being born?" I said.

The paperback jumped out of her hands, and she looked up and grinned, remembering back: two years and two months, more or less. She put out her hands, and I walked through the weeds to take them. They were hot and sweaty from holding the book in the sun.

"People kiss when they haven't seen each other for three solid months," she said.

I dropped down on one knee, which put my lips even with her forehead. Frankly, I'd never kissed a girl before, and I hadn't focused my plans on the forehead. Still, you've got to start someplace. But she lifted her face, and I planted a big wet one right on her nose.

"Polly's right," she sighed as I settled down beside her. "I'll never end up marrying either one of you guys. We've got too long a history together. It really takes all the magic out of it." She wiped the wetness off her nose with the back of her hand.

"You thinking of marriage in the near future?" I inquired.

"Time's passing," she said. "You know we're in high school tomorrow, don't you?"

"No we're not."

"You've really been out of it. The administration pulled one of its switches. They've abolished the junior high system and replaced it with a middle school. It's this educational innovation they've just heard about. So instead of being big ninth-graders at Slocum JHS, we're going to be lowly freshmen in the high school. They've bumped us up to the big time."

"You're making this up." I really hate change.

"No I'm not, and besides, what's wrong with it?" Kate said. "Isn't high school where it's all happening? Don't they have breakdancing in the halls and Duran Duran over the PA? Don't they have darling little cheerleaders in little bitty skirts, spelling out letters with their whole bodies at halftime? And haven't we just been waiting for the day we get there? The day's tomorrow."

"I don't believe this," I said. "My third new school

in three years. This is getting ridiculous. And the horse farm's gone too."

"So we'll have our own shopping mall," Kate said. "Isn't that every teenager's dream?"

"Boy, do I hate change," I said. "Let's not."

She smiled a wise little smile. "I won't if you won't."

It was pretty nice there, the two of us in the warm September sun on the last free day. Very nice. But it was about time to mention Trav. I put it off another minute.

"What are you reading?"

"Lord of the Flies," Kate said. "It's on the freshman summer reading list. Didn't you get yours?"

I pulled up my knees into the well-known fetal position. "I'm definitely not ready for this. Any of it."

"Neither is Trav."

I thought a cloud had crossed the sun, but it was only a change in Kate.

"This high school business has really thrown him. They've got all these different electives, and he's really tense about making the right choices. Really tense."

"Trav's a worried man," I said.

Time skipped a beat. "Is that it?" Kate said. "Is that all there is to Trav? Poor old Trav, he's a worrier. Period."

There was an edge on her voice. I'd ticked her off somehow.

"I don't know," I said. "That's just the way he is. If

he isn't worried about school, he's worried about the Middle East or someplace."

"Did you ever wonder why?"

Probably I hadn't, which I wasn't about to admit. I wondered how to move us out of this. "Where's Trav now?"

"He and his parents flew to Bermuda for the Labor Day weekend. They're due back tonight."

It always amazed me how many places Subs found to go to. And I was supposed to feel sorry for somebody who could fly to Bermuda? It sounded like a great place, wherever it was.

"You know what?" Kate said. "I wasn't going to say anything about this, but I will. I came down here one day this summer, and Trav was already here." She meant this little clearing. It seemed to be their place, Kate and Trav's. That hit me somewhat hard.

"He was already down here," she was saying, "and didn't see me coming. He was pacing up and down, wearing a little track in the weeds. He was working his hands together, wringing them." Kate looked off, remembering. "I thought of Skeeter. Trav was talking to himself, muttering. He was quietly out of control."

"What was worrying him that time?"

"Just listen. They'd taken his dad to the hospital, right from work. They had him in the intensive-care unit. Mrs. Kirby was the only one who could see him. They thought he'd had a heart attack."

"Had he?"

Kate shook her head. "They ran tests, and it was

only stress and overwork. He was back at his office in less than a week."

"Runs in the family," I said, but Kate didn't bother to hear that.

"The point is that Trav didn't know yet—whether his father was going to live or die. And he'd read some article somewhere that there's an epidemic of heart attacks among middle-aged men. He was afraid his father was going to die. He was really afraid of that."

I couldn't see it. "He doesn't even like his dad."

Kate was drawing away from me. I couldn't seem to say the right thing.

"That could make it ten times worse, like he'd be guilty if it happened. What could be worse than wishing you could do something when it's too late? Anyway, you don't have to like somebody to love them."

That was getting too deep for me, so I managed to say another wrong thing. "You never even had a dad, Kate. Has Trav ever bothered to realize that?"

"Have you?" Kate said. "Besides, I have a father somewhere. Mother had to marry him when she was going to have me. She divorced him when I was maybe two minutes old, but I have a father somewhere. The point is, I can get along without him. Trav isn't so sure he could get along without his."

It could really cut down on trips to Bermuda. That was a really low thought, worse than wimpish. At least I kept it to myself.

Instead, I said, "Trav worries about stuff that hasn't happened. He worries about things he can't do anything about. He thinks his folks are leaning on him when actually they're taking him off to Bermuda to calm him down."

Kate pulled up a tuft of dry dandelions. "I know it, and it bothers me because I don't understand what it means. I don't like mysteries. When I start reading them, I always cheat and peek at the last page."

"Maybe Trav isn't that much of a mystery. Maybe this is just his way of, you know, showing off—making a big deal of himself."

"Who to?" Kate said, sharp. "Us? You don't believe that, Buck."

"Well, not to us, maybe."

"Then who? People around school? The other Subs up there in Greenbriar? He doesn't relate enough to them to show off. I wish he did. I wish he wasn't so alone inside himself."

"Maybe he ought to talk to somebody," I said. "A counselor or somebody." It was something to say.

"He has me to talk to," Kate said. "I don't know if it helps, but he has me."

"What does he talk to you about?" I didn't even want to know.

"Sometimes he's just like everybody else, and fun and . . . Trav. But then he sort of goes out of focus. And not just when they took his dad to the hospital. One minute he's being real, and the next minute we're in Afghanistan or Poland and the world's falling apart. Or he's pacing up and down, wondering if he ought to go away to a boarding school to get away from his parents or school or something. He won't go, though. Boarding school might be different, but *he* wouldn't be."

It was like Trav was there in the clearing now, between us, taking over. It was beginning to look more and more like I was in their private space, where I wasn't needed. Kate heard me thinking that. I felt her elbow, sharp in my ribs.

"Don't sulk. It makes your lower lip look all swollen, like that time Skeeter—"

"Never mind," I said. "Never mind."

"Besides, you weren't here all summer. We didn't even have our old foursome for cards. Polly hates three-handed games."

"I'm glad to hear I'm good for something," I said, very bitter.

"So Trav and I came down here a lot."

"I didn't even know this place was here," I said. "How come I didn't know?" I looked around at the orchard-room, very suspicious.

"I thought I'd outgrown it myself," Kate said. "When I was a kid, it was my own little kingdom— queendom. Just being here helps, with all the trees tucked in around you. So I brought Trav down. It's even a great place to feel sorry for yourself, as you're finding out right now."

"What have you two been doing down here?" Little ugly images began to play in my mind.

I was probably lucky she didn't blast me for that.

"You know," she said, "once a long time ago I left my Cabbage Patch doll down here overnight, and it rained. You should have seen the expression on her face the next morning."

She jabbed me in the ribs again. I was supposed to lighten up. I was supposed to smile kindly at this old memory. I tried.

"You look like you've been doing a stretch in jail. Don't they have any sun in Cleveland? You ought to skin off your shirt and get some rays."

So I leaned forward to pull my shirt over my head. I was sweating anyway. But then I stopped. Through the tunnel of my collar, I caught another glimpse of Kate's long brown bare legs.

I just stopped, lost and tangled in my half-off shirt. Kate had seen me shirtless plenty of times, but now it was different. I don't mean I had some big new beefy build to show off. I wish I had. But we were . . . older. Somebody had switched the game plan on us. I had hair under my arms now, and maybe a little acne on my shoulders, nothing too bad. I don't know why, but I couldn't manage to get that shirt off.

I pulled it back on, tucked it into my pants.

"You've changed," Kate said. "Things do."

CHAPTER SEVEN

High school was a whole new experience. The first week was chaos, which they called Orientation, and it went down from there. People milled around for weeks like fear-crazed cattle. These were the teachers. We, the students, spent September standing in the gym, waiting for various room assignments. Everybody tried to look as bored as possible to keep personal panic under control.

For one thing, we were suddenly a four-year school in a building designed for three. For another, a new neighborhood called The Meadows of Greenbriar had opened up, a major complex that seemed to spring up overnight like toadstools.

Dad had been working over there, but you didn't notice the place happening. They had to cut in whole new roads to the route, and the traffic for miles around was getting lethal. All these new kids were suddenly in school, and a percentage of them looked like they'd come out of the audience for *Saturday Night Live*.

The Subs were still maintaining their position and their Izod–and–L.L. Bean image. On a clear day you could still make out a few authentic Slos, the polyester people. But now we had punk. We had funk. We had New Wave. We had Culture Club. We had some people walking around who looked like they'd been thrown out of a Billy Idol concert.

A new name cropped up for this category of crazies. They were called Spaces, for space cadets, I guess. So now we had Slos, Subs, and Spaces, and still I didn't know who I was.

Of course, we had girls too: big, beautiful girls from all over. The major look filtering down from the seniors was a designer label by the name of Guess? It was a cross between combat fatigues and farmers' denim, all worn as wrinkled as possible with strategic parts left exposed. You'd catch some fairly memorable glimpses of girls wearing baggy bib overalls over see-through work shirts with cartridge belts hanging off their hips. All natural fibers and top-grain leathers.

The Guess? people at the top of the line looked a lot like the Pine Hill Slos down at the bottom who'd been having to wear this type gear all along except with different labels.

Speaking of Pine Hill, Skeeter was back.

He'd been promoted. They don't like to scar any of us with failure, and high school was giving him whole new opportunities. There wasn't too much doubt about who'd unbolted the gym bleachers or who set the lumber-room fire in Industrial Arts. I personally began to think Skeeter had his own set of school keys for night work.

There were some enormous guys in school, real creatures who were bigger than Skeeter was ever going to get. But he kept out of their way and found various other projects for himself. The place was, I repeat, chaos.

Kate and Trav and I got together after school on that first day. We had to make a point of doing that, what with the turmoil. I hadn't seen either of them all day, but I suspected they'd kept track of each other. Anyway, we were all three there at Kate's. We'd had it up to here with Orientation.

"Disorientation," Kate said, "and more of the same tomorrow."

Trav had a great Bermuda tan, but he looked pale under it. He was topping out at almost six feet, and it looked to me like he'd lost some weight. The web belt holding up his pants about lapped him twice. He looked older. His eyebrows were heavier or something. There were little hollows under his cheekbones.

At school it was a new year, but back on Polly's porch it was still summertime: warm, dusty, pollinated. The yard was drying up, and the orchard leaves rustled. Kind of a bittersweet time. I thought maybe we could get back to normal there.

Kate was shelling peas into a pan, and I was halfway helping her, collecting pods. Trav was thumbing through the high school handbook. We were sitting down on the step, and Polly was on the porch above us, looking like Mount Rushmore, with her chair always trained on the orchard. She wasn't missing a word.

Trav couldn't turn loose of the handbook. He was still trying to second-guess all the elective courses they offered. In social studies alone they had World Cultures, Politics and Government, Contemporary Social Issues, and I forget what all. When sign-up time came, I covered my eyes and picked something.

They had foreign languages, too, which I wasn't going near. But Trav was trying to work in both German and French, not to mention trigonometry, which was eleventh-grade level. Over the summer he'd taken correspondence courses in algebra and geometry. Long division is my outer limit.

"They ought to have had a summer-school session," Trav was muttering. "They're throwing us into a no-win situation, and from now on everything is going right on the transcript that the colleges see. We're going to be taking SATs before we know what's happening."

I considered asking him what SATs are, but decided against it. I had the feeling that after we all got squared away, high school wasn't going to be that different.

"For one thing," I said, "they moved Sherrie Slater up to the high school with us." I'd noticed her around, clutching a new grade book, teetering along through the mobs on her high heels, as lost as any of us.

"Yes," Kate said. "I wonder why they did that."

"She wasn't hacking it in junior high teaching," I said. "Maybe they're giving her a second chance on a new level."

"Somehow that doesn't seem like administration thinking," Kate said. "At least they didn't stick her with a freshman homeroom. She doesn't have to start her day with Skeeter."

"Maybe they're setting her up for failure, so they can fire her," I said.

"That sounds about right," said Kate.

"Why are they scheduling French I and German I in the same period?" Trav said, never looking up from the handbook. "Why do they do things like that?"

"What a bunch of worrywarts," said Polly Prior.

Kate finished up with the peas, and I took a handful of pods to throw out over in the long grass. When I came back, she was sitting closer to Trav, trying to get his nose out of that handbook. Her technique was to rest her hand in a very friendly way on his knee. It was a perfectly reasonable thing to be doing. I hated it.

She was getting his mind off school by talking about the summer. It seems they'd done a lot of things together, maybe more than they were mentioning. Trav's mom played golf at Breezy Knoll Country Club, so they had pool privileges there. They were talking about that. It tended to explain Kate's great tan. If you took away the peas and the porch, she could almost pass as a Sub.

She was getting Trav to remember the lifeguard at

the pool who looked like he didn't want to get his hair wet. It was real sharing time for two of us. Somehow there didn't look like a lot of room for me on the porch step with them. Maybe Polly noticed me looming there with my hands in my hip pockets. Maybe she noticed, but they didn't seem to.

"Who's for a little game of chance?" Polly said. "Won't take but a minute to set up the table."

"Not for me, Polly," I said. "I got to be going."

"What's your hurry?"

"I got to work out my elective choices," I said, oozing with irony. I strolled off around the side of the house, chin up and very cool in case anybody happened to be watching.

I know I was overreacting. I halfway knew it at the time. But it seemed pretty obvious that Kate and Trav were turning into a couple, and I was truly ticked off. I was so ticked off, I went out for freshman football. I must have been looking for a new team or something. I must have been out of my mind.

The PE department was more chaotic than the rest of the school. They'd never had freshman football before because they'd never had freshmen, and it takes less than this to confuse a coach. Anyway, they posted notices all over school to turn out. That's how I happened to be sitting practically naked on a bench down in the locker room with a row of equally unpromising ninth-grade gridiron hopefuls.

Coach Simca looked less hopeful, but he gave us a

halfhearted pep talk about sportsmanship, keeping ourselves clean in all ways, and pass patterns.

"You men are in incredibly poor shape," he'd say, scratching his big, sweat-shirted belly. "You men have got a phenomenal amount of catching up to do."

All we did was calisthenics, not even wind sprints, and on our own time. We practiced after school at the far end of the field to keep out of the way of the real team. That was okay with me, because even at a distance the varsity squad looked like a tree full of King Kongs. You could hear their war cries from far off.

We had to pay for our shoes, and we were suited up in practice gear: shorts, athletic department T-shirts, oversize helmets. We looked like a bunch of dandelions out there, weedy and heavy-headed, jumping around through tractor tires. I lasted three days, so I'll never know what position they might have played me at. Probably blocking dummy.

After the first day I told Dad what I'd done. After all, I had to keep training hours, so I was pulling out the Hide-A-Bed to be in it and officially asleep by nine-thirty. I asked Dad if he'd gone out for football. With that build, I supposed they'd probably drafted him.

He shook his head and said, "I always liked making my own plans."

Then on day two of practice, something fairly remarkable happened. The freshman team acquired its own cheerleaders. At least, this group of six or

seven girls turned up on the sidelines. The real
cheerleaders were practicing in front of the empty
stands many yards away, so this was a splinter group
of some kind. They weren't even close to being the
same size and were wearing quite a variety of their
own clothes. They looked leaderless to me.

As we were jumping through tires and dropping
for push-ups, we'd notice them. They were working
out routines in a group, then spreading out for some
ragged high kicks and leaps. You could hear them,
just little twitterings on the breeze.

> *"We're the Greenbriar Aces,*
> *Going through our paces. . . ."*

Somehow I'd thought the name of this school was
Slocum Township HS. But maybe that was too
cornball a name for them. The cheers, and the legs,
were distracting, and Simca had to keep after us with
his whistle.

Around four o'clock we were taking our break, just
milling around, drinking out of dippers, keeping our
helmets in the crooks of our arms, because there's
this unwritten rule about never letting your helmet
hit the ground unless your head's in it.

Anyway, one of the girls breaks off from her group
and heads over toward us. Several of us noticed this
big, rangy redhead who I'd have taken for a senior.
Creamy pale forehead, gigantic eyes under visible
lashes. Quite a figure—almost too much. When she
moved, she moved all over. She was a definite Space,
but she wore a uniform all her own.

A Boy George–type shirt, a double-wrapped belt over Guess? jeans, and very pointy elf boots. She was somewhere left of New Wave, and she was heading straight for me.

She stepped up, blocking out the world. "Where's the beef?"

Why me? That was all I could think. Why me?

"Is this Wussyville or what?" the girl said.

"Well, it's only the freshman—"

"I'm not talking just the team," she said. "I'm talking the entire school. Is this place Middle Earth or what? Are you new here too?"

"Well, I'm a freshman," I said.

"So am I. But I mean, where do you come from?"

Somehow I didn't think Farnham would ring any bells with her.

"Because I'm from California," she said, "so I'm flexible. But this whole area is pretty much out of the question. I mean, half this school's so stuck up, you can't believe it, and the other half looks like Amateur Night at a chicken-plucking contest. Give me a break."

Her gaze dropped down. I noticed a lot of makeup on her lashes. She seemed to be checking out my legs. I shifted my helmet around in front.

"Are you, ah, going to be cheerleaders for . . . us?"

"Whatever," she said. "A bunch of us just got together and decided to come out, mainly as a hoot." She jerked her head to the other girls, who were hanging in together. The sunlight glinted gold in her coppery curls.

"I guess you'll need a sponsor," I said.

"Like an adult to supervise us? Forget that. In California we don't have adults." She lowered her voice then, but she could still be heard in Pine Hill. "Frankly, I don't have much hope for your team. It looks like everybody ought to be cut from it. Half of them haven't cleared puberty yet."

Around us my teammates seemed frozen in position. Nothing moved but her mouth.

"Don't go by me, though. I'm from California, so I've got my standards. I'm from surfer country, so I'm practically burned out on babes."

Babes? "Babes?"

"You know, babes," she said. "That's what we call guys in California."

"Oh."

I happened to notice that her ears were pierced three—no, four times on each side. She had various little dangly earrings climbing up both her lobes.

"You're okay, though. You're as close to a hunk as they've got. I saw you right away." She made big eyes at me, great big ones. They were hazel with little flecks in them. I could feel my entire body going beet red. But you couldn't call her unfriendly. Whether she was putting me on or not was anybody's guess.

The coach's whistle split the air, and the girl began to dance away, sideways, in a takeoff on a cheer being led. Legs apart, legs together. Legs apart, legs together. What had Kate said about cheerleaders? That they spell out letters with their whole bodies.

"By the way, what's your name?" she said, so I told her. "Mine's Hazenfield. My first name's Antoinette, but everybody calls me Rusty." She pointed to her head. "Rusty Hazenfield. Got that?"

Got it.

"So I'll see you around, okay?" She was still dancing sideways away, waving invisible pom-poms and yelling back. "You know, anytime. I'm flexible."

The whistle went again, and we scrambled back onto the tires. I took my time getting my helmet back on and hid my face in it till it stopped feeling so red.

On the third day, practice was over for me before it got a good start. We'd just come out of the locker room, and I figured if we were going to have cheerleaders, I ought to start looking good. I was warming up with squat-jumps and trying to get into it. I'd pulled the chin strap on my helmet extra tight to bunch up my face so I'd look like a mean and lean machine.

There on the sidelines appeared a pair of familiar figures, Kate and Trav. Kate was shielding her eyes with her hand and scanning the field. Then she picked me out.

"I don't believe this," I heard her say distinctly. "Buck! Get over here." She sounded like somebody's mother. She was even pointing to the ground right in front of herself.

So I ambled over. Sweat was already beginning to trickle down my face from under the hot helmet. I thought it might make me look somewhat jockish and wished I had black smudges rubbed in under my eyes for the final touch.

"How's it going?" I planted my hands on my lean and mean hips.

"Have you lost your mind," Kate greeted me. "That helmet looks like a *growth.*"

Trav just gazed at my heavy, globular head. "What's this all about, Buck?" he asked in a calm and reasoning voice.

"Going out for football?" I said. "Why not? It's football season."

"Are you trying to get yourself killed?" Kate said, ticked off once more. "Are you trying to turn yourself into a *paraplegic?*"

I didn't take that too kindly. "Listen, I weigh a hundred and forty-one pounds. Compared to most of these guys, I'm Mr. T."

"And you smell like old gym shoes." Kate's nose wrinkled dramatically. "Have you been wearing that same shirt every day?"

"We don't change our clothes till our first winning game," I explained. "No laundry till a win. It's a tradition."

"A *tradition?*" Kate clutched her forehead. "How can freshmen have a tradition? We just got here. Have you already had a head injury? I'm serious." She was beginning to stamp on the chalk-marked grass. "Is this where you've been after school in the afternoons? We didn't even *think* to look for you here. We gave you credit for a little more sense than that."

So they'd been looking for me, had they? Maybe that's why I'd gone out for the team in the first place. That thought just crossed my mind. But Kate was hopping mad. She could fly off the handle quicker than anybody I ever knew.

"You don't even *like* football, and do you know how dumb you look out there with all these other *clones?*"

Trav put his hand on her shoulder to cool her down, but she shrugged away from him. I noticed that too. These were my friends, and I couldn't seem to remember why I'd walked away from them.

"Buck, if you really want to go out for football, fine," Trav said. He spoke low, which was a nice change from Kate, who could get somewhat screechy. "But it's pretty time-consuming, and we'd miss having you around. It wouldn't be the same."

Time-consuming. It was a perfect Trav term, but I knew what he meant. I started grinning, and so did he, over Kate's head.

For some reason I was wearing this helmet, and it weighed a ton. I loosened the chin strap. The idea of two hours of heavy effort every afternoon needed rethinking. I eased the helmet off my head and set it down on the ground, breaking the unbreakable rule. This seemed to solve everything. Then I just put up my somewhat spindly arms.

"Take me," I told them. "I'm yours."

Kate let out a loud sigh of relief, and Trav shifted

his heavy load of books onto his bony hip. We strolled away from my gridiron career.

But first I had to detour down to the locker room to shower and change. When I came back out, they were waiting. Together. Standing close. A sharp jab of the old jealousy attacked my vitals. I fought it.

Also I happened to notice that our volunteer cheerleaders had reappeared out by the field and were doing their stuff. In the long, low rays of the sun I thought I caught a glimpse of red curls glinting.

Still a little damp from the shower, I strolled over to Kate and Trav. "In a way it's a shame," I said. "I'd have looked great in shoulder pads."

"Oh, shut up," said Kate.

CHAPTER EIGHT

It was the three of us again facing freshman year together, but somehow school didn't add up to much. I admit I didn't give my elective courses deep thought, but you ended up with a pretty strange schedule no matter how you played it. Mine looked like a salad bar. I had typing, technical drawing, biology, bonehead math, Contemporary Social Issues.

Something went wrong with the computer that programmed us, because Trav and I ended up having English together. He was supposed to be in something advanced, like Shakespeare for Geniuses. But there we were in the same class, which looked like a dumping ground to me.

Trav was unhappy, really unhappy. At least we didn't have Contemporary Social Issues together. I was relieved, because it was all about the deteriorating world situation, and that could really get Trav going.

Then the English teacher walked in, and it was Sherrie Slater. You could tell right there that high school teaching wasn't going to be any better for her. The minute she hit the door, all the girls groaned. Kate said it was the same in her class. Kate had Sherrie, too, but in a different period.

I was kind of glad to see her again. It brought back the old days, and she was really pretty. She wore blue eyeliner, not too much, and there were guys in the room who kept records on how many days she left the top button on her blouse unbuttoned. When she turned to the chalkboard, you could see the outline of the back part of her bra.

She wasn't trying to drive us crazy. She just wasn't cut out for teaching. And she wouldn't have minded being our friend, which is fatal. Also, when she found out that all of us had already read *Johnny Tremain* in eighth grade, she looked pretty lost.

Sherrie talked in a low, somewhat breathy voice that didn't work either. In the first week she said, "I thought we might spend the first ten minutes of every period just writing in our notebooks."

Eyes rolled all over the room.

"Just getting down our thoughts in an undirected way."

She settled onto the corner of her desk, but it hiked her skirt, so she edged back.

"Through writing we can begin to . . . catch glimpses of ourselves. Nature too. Our impressions." She glanced out the window, but it was blacktopped parking lot. "I won't look at what you write unless you'd like me to. I won't grade them."

That about closed the case on her in the first week.

Who's going to do anything if a grade isn't involved anyway? Trav slid down in his chair, flipped open his German book, and began to underline things in it. He walled her out. Everybody did, and class went downhill from there.

Except with Trav for English, I was lost in a sea of strangers. I even got stuck with the wrong lunch period and had to eat by myself. Again, I had this clear picture of Trav and Kate in the cafeteria together every noon while I was in another wing, discovering technical drawing.

It was always rush hour in the halls, but Rusty Hazenfield was impossible to miss. You always had some warning because you could see her coming. She was as tall as most guys, and she had eyes on her like sealed-beam headlights. For every day she had a different costume, and she carried her books in a beach bag.

Occasionally she'd block my path. Rusty never forgot a face.

"Honestly," she'd say, "is this place the Temple of Doom or what? This school is a trip. I mean, people don't even know you're here. They'll walk right over you. They can't *see* you if they didn't know you before. These people are androids."

She'd bat her lashes at me, and they were liable to be any color you can name. I thought I might as well try a little conversation, even though she did fine all on her own.

"So how are the freshman cheerleaders shaping up, Rusty?"

All the dangle-bangles in her ears rattled, and her big hazel eyes popped. "You mean you don't know? It should have been on TV. When the Official Pep Squad bothered to notice we were there, they had us abolished by the PE department. Can you believe it? And that's what they call themselves, too: the *Official* Pep Squad.

"Could you puke on your boots? And I don't care if they are mostly juniors and seniors, have you had a look at them? Half of them are anorexics. They shouldn't be trying to lift pom-poms. They should be under a doctor's care. How come you didn't know?"

"I'm off the team."

"Not *cut*. That would be so *demeaning*."

"I quit. Honest."

She nodded with closed eyes. "Who could blame you? That whole team was a bunch of Muppets. I'm flexible myself, but there are limits."

The hallway was clearing out by then, just before the bell.

"Bells," said Rusty Hazenfield, "always with the bells. In California we could care less."

Then she'd be gone till the next time, swinging her beach bag, swinging her everything. One thing I noticed about Rusty: She always seemed to be breaking out of a crowd of friends to come over and talk to you. But actually that crowd of friends wasn't there.

Over the next weeks they began trying to whip up our enthusiasm for Homecoming. I don't know who they expected to come back for it, this being a virtually new school. But the first two assemblies were all about the upcoming game, the halftime parade with floats, the bonfire, the dance. For the dance we were supposed to come up with costumes to represent various periods of Slocum Township history. The halls were being decorated with orange and black crepe paper, which were either the school colors or for Halloween; nobody quite knew.

"It's just a device to draw all the diverse student factions together," Trav said, "and the historical period costumes are to give us instant roots. The administration learns these group-dynamics techniques at seminars. And they've scheduled Homecoming over Halloween weekend, presumably to cut down on vandalism. My dad . . ." Trav's voice trailed off. Mr. Kirby had just been elected president of the school board, and Trav was none too happy about that either.

Anyway, it was getting close to Homecoming because the school was completely orange and black. Trav wasn't in great shape. I think they were keeping him busy enough in German and maybe chemistry, but he'd about had it with everything else.

One day when we were swinging into English he said, "I'm going to talk to her. This is pointless."

"Who?" I said. "What?" I was always a step behind, but he was really just talking to himself anyway. He dumped his books on me and headed for Sherrie Slater's desk.

We were early, so nobody else had come in. She was sitting there twisting the ring on her finger and staring down at her blotter. Her mind was some-

where else. She had honey-colored hair, and it fell
forward so you couldn't see all her face. Usually she
had a smile for you, but she didn't look up till Trav
was standing over her. I didn't know whether to go
down the aisle to my desk or what. I hovered.

"Ms. Slater?" Still, I thought she wasn't going to
look up, but then she did.

"Oh. Trav. What?"

"You busy?"

She shook her head and put her hand down on her
desk. When she looked up at him, a curl of her hair
stayed on her cheek.

Trav was still losing weight. I could have sworn it.
Even his Ivy League dress shirt was drooping off his
shoulders, and he looked taller and narrower than
ever.

"Ms. Slater, why are we here?"

She didn't get it. Neither did I exactly. Little soft
furrows appeared in her forehead.

"I mean, what's supposed to be going on here?"
Trav's voice wavered, but he smoothed it out,
pitched it at her.

"What's English class for? We're supposed to read
great writers and analyze their ideas, aren't we? Instead we read these little condensations out of the
textbook. Most of us don't read them at all. You read
them aloud to us in class, and then you ask us how we
like them."

Sherrie Slater drew in her lower lip, bit it. She did
that sometimes.

"And we're supposed to write, aren't we?" Trav

said. "We're supposed to learn grammar, develop a style. We're supposed to learn how to do research and use it—footnote it. We're going to have to know these things for college."

The color was rising on his neck. He was heating up. He did that when he thought people weren't hearing him.

"But you're a very good student," Sherrie Slater said. "You're excellent, Trav."

"How would you know?" He was almost bending over her now. "How would you know? I'm coasting. We're all coasting. This is recess."

She looked away from him, out across the empty rows. The halls outside were full and loud, but we were trapped in this vacuum. I was wishing people would come in and this would stop.

"There are people in the class," she said, "who don't have your abilities, Trav, and they—"

"Then they need work too," he said, getting louder. He jammed his hands down on her desk, grinding the heels of them into the metal top. "We're losing time. I know the rest of them don't care, but they're losing. We're not getting any better. We're not getting anywhere."

I thought he was going to reach for her. His hand clenched. I don't mean he wanted to hit her, but he wanted to hit something. I knew what he meant. I didn't feel it, but I knew what he meant. Sherrie Slater moved her chair an inch away. It had wheels and they squeaked. Her hand slipped off the desk. She was pulling back, which was the wrong direction.

I didn't mean to be looking at her at all, but I noticed her eyes were wet, filling with tears.

Then I saw the piece of paper in front of her. I'd moved up on them, closer. The paper on her desk had been through a Xerox machine. I couldn't make out what was on it. Just big blots and scratchings, like a kid's drawing. She looked aside at me, and both her hands came out to cover it. But they stopped and dropped into her lap.

All this time Trav was looming over her, and she was feeling the heat, taking it. The tears spilled out and down her face. All of a sudden, a lot of them. She just let them run.

"And the SATs," Trav was saying. "We're going to have vocabulary lists. You either know them or you don't. We need to get ready for that. Junior year's not that far away. You can't start studying for SATs the night before or even the year before. You've got to—"

"Trav." I had to say something because he wasn't seeing. He was only looking at himself. "Trav, ease off."

He looked around, because he'd forgotten I was there. I nodded to Sherrie Slater. She put her hand over her eyes, and the tears were spilling out around her fingers. They were blue tears, from her eyeliner.

Then he saw. "What is it? What did I say? I was only trying . . ."

She had both hands over her face now. She wasn't sobbing, and in a way it was worse. I really wished I could do something. Then I got another look at the paper on her desk, and I just picked it up. She didn't notice, or maybe she just let me.

They were hands. Somebody had stuck his hands into a copier machine and Xeroxed them. They were these big, animal-paw hands black-blotted on the white page. I must have known right then whose hands they were, even before I read the scratchy words grease-penciled in underneath:

I GOING TO HAVE THESE HANDS
ALL OVER YOR BODY

I really knew then.

I held the page in front of Trav so he couldn't miss it. He was pretty riled up, but seeing Sherrie Slater dissolve in front of him had an effect, when he could manage to see it. Now I had something else for him. He looked at the page without touching it. I made sure he read the words too.

"Skeeter," I said, just to make it clear.

Sherrie Slater's hands came down. She pulled open a drawer to get her purse out, and a handkerchief. People were coming in for class now, behind us. Trav and I formed a little screen between her and them. I folded the Xerox paper over in half.

She found her handkerchief, balled it up, and made quick swipes down her cheeks. Her eyes really looked trapped. She gave us a half smile to move us off, but she looked bad, wiped out. I don't think anybody in the room was involved enough to notice. I took the folded paper. I took Skeeter's hands away from her.

When I walked off down the aisle ahead of Trav, I heard him behind me.

"I've got to get out of here," he said. "I've got to get out of all this."

I thought he was talking about going away to boarding school again. Or to a private school. Some Subs did. I don't know what I thought.

When I met Kate in the hall, I showed Skeeter's hands to her. Trav wasn't around. I sort of blamed him for giving Sherrie Slater a shove when she was right there on the edge anyway. I showed the paper to Kate, and I didn't know how she'd react. I'd thought of throwing it away.

She went white, white as the paper. She knew whose work it was, and I told her who he'd meant it for. Kate took the page and held it by the edges. She wasn't hopping mad. She was somewhere past that.

"Give it to me," she said, but she already had it. Then she walked away like we hadn't even met.

It was one day the next week that the announcement over the PA called Sherrie Slater out of class during English. After a while we noticed a cop car outside in the parking lot. The principal was out there and so was Sherrie, talking to a trooper. They were all congregated around the empty space where she usually parked her car.

There were a lot of rumors, but it came down to this. Somebody had hot-wired her Chevy Citation, and the cops had found it in the parking lot at K Mart, tireless, and with its upholstery slashed.

CHAPTER NINE

Early in Homecoming week, Kate got busy organizing us. We'd stretched summer as far as it would go. Now we were in Polly's kitchen instead of hanging out on the back porch. We were drinking cider out of juice glasses. The cider jug was on the floor next to Polly's wheelchair, where she could reach it for refills.

Trav was there. He was mad at the world by then: at the pointless classes and the blank faces in the school halls and the violence oozing in around the edges. But Kate was holding us together. She was full of plans. Some we knew. Some we didn't.

"The thing is," she said, "we're practically down to the wire when it comes to costumes. And they have to be authentic Slocum Township costumes too." She meant the Homecoming dance after the bonfire, and she was really talking it up.

"If I go, I go like this." I was in my usual: Sears jeans and a plaid flannel shirt I wore over a thermal-underwear top because I thought it made my arms look bigger.

Kate shot me a glance full of meaning. "Well, either I figure out a costume or I don't go. And if I go in costume, you guys—"

"Count me out," I said.

"Me too," Trav said, "really."

Kate's eyes slewed over to Polly, who was picking up everything.

"Oh, well, where am I going to find a historical costume anyhow? Might as well forget it. I guess I don't even want to go."

Polly's chin was cradled in her brittle old hand. She was deep in thought. Then her hands dropped down to her wheels. "Come on," she said. "Let's us go to my room."

Kate slumped with the effort of priming Polly. Kate had a scheme. It wasn't like her to get carried away over a school event. We never needed anybody to organize our lives. She was involving Polly, which made sense, because she liked to keep Polly involved. And she was nailing Trav and me down for Homecoming, making extra sure we'd be there. In fact, she was overdoing. This thought skated past my mind, but that's as far as I got with it.

Though Polly didn't let people into her room, she was scooting there now. I helped her get her chair over the doorsills. The room was on the first floor because Kate couldn't get her up and down stairs.

I guess it had been the parlor once. It had a combination of smells, some good, some not so good.

"All you could see out that window at one time was the level line of the horizon." Polly pointed at a window with the shade pulled down. "This was country then, real country. People knew you."

Polly'd lived a long time, and she hadn't thrown out anything yet. It could have been a flea market, and I'm just talking about what you could see.

"Now, don't you kids touch anything." She was wheeling around the room, checking on things, showing it off. "I got everything the way I want it."

She had everything all right. Clocks in all shapes, funeral parlor fans stuck into the mirror frame, a fish tank full of old-time purses, hats of various eras on her bedposts, pillows with mottos, sea shells and perfume bottles, framed pictures of people so faded, they were just barely there.

Trav didn't know what to make of it. He liked everything neat and orderly. The place even closed in on me, and I live in a trailer.

"Ain't this a bunch of stuff?" said Polly Prior. "This is my life in here."

She was different in her room. Not younger. She was at her youngest with us around the card table. Here she was ancient with all her life stretched back to another century. She wanted to show us things and explain. Her hand looked transparent when she reached out for a picture or a little dance program or something. She'd find things, too, things she hadn't noticed lately.

"Oh, looky there," she'd say, and find something else.

Polly'd forgotten why we were there, why she'd let us in. But Kate waited. In some things Kate could be

as patient as she needed to be. Then Polly remembered. She wheeled over to an old golden oak bureau
and started pulling out the drawers.

I thought she'd spill herself out of her chair, but she
said, "No, I got it. I got it."

She was clawing through layers of things, folded
clothes and quilts, many layers. She pulled up a long
string of pearls and said, "Oh, I was hot stuff in my
time. You just don't know."

Her little old pink eyes were bright inside the spec-
tacles, and her old baldy head poked way down in the
drawers. She was having herself a time.

"Where is it? I seen it here a while back." Then her
old crooked fingers rustled through tissue paper, and
she pulled up a dress. She held it up as high as she
could reach, but the skirt on it was still coming out of
the drawer. Turning in her chair, she held it up to
Kate.

I can't describe it. It had been pink once. The
sleeves were like wings, and there was a lot of elabo-
rate beadwork on the front. Kate took it from her and
held it against herself. The skirt went all the way to
the floor.

"That'll do for you, Katie," she said, and you could
see it would.

In the corner of the room stood a screen plastered
over with old postcards and valentines. Kate went
behind it.

"That was my high school graduation dress," Polly
said. "Wasn't but three of us in the class. Two of us
girls and a boy. He was my brother. He was older

than me, but I was two years ahead of myself in
school and graduated at sixteen. I was right smart."

She put her hand up against her cheek and said, "I
had my diploma here, I forget just where," and she
looked around the room, around her life, for her diploma.

Then Kate was there, in the dress. She'd changed
with lightning speed, and now she was beside the
screen, very still. Trav saw her first. I think he
stopped breathing. Then I saw her. Then Polly. She
made a little sound at the sight of Kate, a little cry,
and her hands fell into a heap in her lap. What little
hair she had was pulled back into a knot on the back
of her head. It rested against the hump of her shoulders as she looked up at Kate.

The dress fitted perfectly. Except she wasn't Kate
anymore. She was a picture in an old frame. Her hair
was the same, smooth and tucked back behind her
ears and a little bit tangled from putting the dress on.
But she was somebody else. The arms in the wispy
sleeves, the shape of her inside the dress. Even her
face somehow. She never wore any makeup, and it
worked, and it was still working.

"Me," Polly said.

She went back in her mind, and maybe we went
with her. It was quiet, and the room smelled like
lavender from the drawers. Then Polly's head jerked
up. "Now for you boys," she said. "Let me think."

After a lot of rummaging, she located a huge box
like a footlocker behind a stack of *National Ge-
ographic*s. "You, Trav," she said.

Humoring her, I guess, he dragged the box behind the screen. Polly got busy, digging around to find the fan that went with Kate's dress. But Kate stood quietly, running her hands down the sides of the skirts. They were like cobwebs, layers of them.

I tried to see Polly on the day she'd worn it. Country-girl Polly going off to her three-person graduation exercises in a wagon, maybe, over the rutted roads. I could smell the clover in the ditch and the turned earth in the fields. But Polly's world had shrunk. They were blacktopping the county road outside, working overtime to get it done before the first freeze.

The screen spoke. Invisible Trav said, "There's a lot to this. I'm not sure how it all works." He was taking too much time to suit Polly.

"You, Buck, I got just the thing for you. Crawl in under my bed and get that big box right agin' the wall." So I went burrowing in, setting off dust storms. It was another treasure cave under there, and I spent a good ten minutes finding a big, bulging box and getting it out.

When I was back on my feet, the room was dead silent. Trav was there, and Polly and Kate were seeing him. He was in a uniform, khaki, World War I. It was loose on him, but the Sam Browne belt slanting across his chest gave it a fit. The high collar came up to his chin, and the pants were full on the sides. His Docksides were still on his feet, but his legs were wrapped around with brown wool bands up to his knees. On his head was a high-crowned, wide-brimmed khaki hat with a leather lanyard for a band. It shadowed his face so he could have been anybody. He looked like an old recruiting poster.

He stood almost at attention, and Polly's hand was up in the air, reaching out to him.

"Harold," she said. "My brother." Behind the moon-shaped glasses her eyes were wild and young —hopeful.

Kate spoke then. She didn't want the moment to be too much for Polly. "What's yours, Buck?"

Mine was a fur coat, pretty ratty, with bald patches.

"Raccoon," Polly said. "Boys wore them at one time, I forget just when."

I put it on, and it swept the floor. Then I did a small Michael Jackson move to see if I could maneuver. The thing was heavy as lead, and I smelled like a giant mothball. It got a laugh out of them, though, even Trav.

"What you need with that," Polly said, "is a pair of wide trousers and one of them porkpie hats."

I had other plans.

Kate went out then, floating in the dress, to get her Instamatic to take some pictures. She knew Polly would want them. They'd be in color, and all the other pictures in the room were gray. When she came back, Polly said, "I had a picture of my brother, Harold, taken down in the orchard on the day he went off to war. Let's us go down to the orchard."

Kate looked across her at Trav and me. Polly wanted to go to the orchard, and maybe she'd forgotten she couldn't walk. She couldn't have been down there in years. I nodded, and so did Trav. We'd get her down there if she wanted to go.

The days were shorter, and it was nearly evening. Between us, Trav and I could lift Polly in her chair down the porch step. The yard was uneven but not too bad. The orchard was trickier, but Polly wanted to go. She edged forward in the chair, rocking like a kid. Kate had tied a scarf around her head and made her wear mittens. The mittened hands were trying to help us. She was about spinning her wheels.

When we got into long grass, we could skim over some of it if we could get the fallen limbs out of the way. Kate came along behind, ducking branches, making girllike cries when her dress got caught on twigs.

It was dark in the orchard rows. The leaves were mostly down, too, clogging the wheels. I don't know how we looked. A vintage soldier and a raccoon and a girl out of a time warp, struggling along to get an old lady in a wheelchair deeper and deeper into a played-out pear orchard. Otherworldly.

We came to Kate's clearing, and it always surprised me how near it was. Polly seemed to know it, so maybe it had always been there. She settled back in her chair. It was cold, but she wouldn't let on. Dark, too, but we had the flash for the pictures. Polly posed us and took the pictures herself. She stripped off her mittens and sighted into the camera through her old spectacle lens.

Mine wasn't going to look like much, just a big

furry form emerging from the trees with a small head on top. But when the flash went on Kate, you could tell it would be great. The pink dress was cut low on her shoulders against the dark, branchy background. And Kate rose up out of the weeds on a pillar of skirt. Great.

Then Trav. He stood really at attention now. I don't know if he was getting a kick out of this. I think maybe he was: being somebody else. He was a toy soldier left behind by kids playing outdoors. When the flash went, it was ghostly. He was there, and then he was gone. Trav, lost in time.

Then one more, Kate and Trav together, because their outfits matched. Just before the flash, she turned to him, took his uniformed arm, and looked up at him, almost clinging. Who were they? A soldier and his girl in 1917 or whenever? Polly seeing her brother off to war? Kate and Trav? It was just the two of them and nothing else, not even the world.

I'd had about enough. It was cold down there and getting late. It was ridiculous. What were we doing there, anyway? I wanted out.

But Polly lingered another minute. It was darker after the flashes. There were only red streaks left in the sky. We were down in a well of trees, and you could see the first stars and the rising moon. Polly looked around her orchard, turning in her chair. I guess she must have been memorizing it.

It was too late in the season to go back to football, so I sulked for a day. So let the soldier and his girl go to the dance. What did they need with me? And who needed Homecoming? And who cared, anyway? Then I went to K Mart.

"What have you got there?" Dad said. We were eating in that night, and he was dragging a couple Swanson TV dinners out of the oven.

"I wanted fur," I said, "but all they had was rubber." I pulled a collapsed gorilla head out of the sack. Not just a mask, the whole head. With eye holes for seeing and snout holes for breathing and big fangs for show. Nice, sloping forehead too.

"What do you get when you cross a raccoon with a gorilla?"

"I give up," Dad said.

"Me."

Now I needed a date.

CHAPTER TEN

"We don't," Rusty Hazenfield said, "ever. Not in California, I mean. We never date. It's too 1950's. I mean, it can tie up a whole evening. It's like a commitment."

I'd figured out where her locker was and happened to be there waiting for her after school. Now she and I were heading down the county road to Kate's house. Kate and Trav would already be there, expecting me. They weren't expecting Rusty Hazenfield. I, too, could make plans. Why not bring Rusty into our Homecoming arrangements? Why not even up the sides.

"It's not exactly a date, Rusty," I said. "It'll be more like the four of us hanging out."

"Four?"

"You and me, Kate and Trav."

"The buttoned-down guy and the girl who's sort of wholesome?" Rusty spoke in a thoughtful voice. "I've seen the three of you around. I wondered what it meant."

"It means we're friends," I said, "but we're . . . flexible." I noticed I wasn't exactly having to drag Rusty along, though she wasn't much of a pedestrian.

"In California," she said, "we only walk on the beach."

When we made our entrance into Polly's kitchen, we created a small sensation. Nobody moved.

"Oh, hi," Rusty said, making right for Kate. "We're in English together, right?"

"Right," said Kate, gazing past her at me.

Rusty shifted to Trav. "Seen you around. Trav, right?" She turned her blinding headlight eyes on him. He blinked. About then she caught her first glimpse of Polly between them, down around the level of their elbows. Polly was gazing up, grinning like a jack-o'-lantern. She likes surprises. Have I mentioned she has a gold tooth, right in front? She does. She was all gold tooth and moon glasses and a couple of wisps of white hair. That first sight of her really slowed Rusty down while Kate remembered her manners.

"This is my great-grandmother, P—Mrs. Prior."

Polly grinned up at Rusty and reached down for the jug. "Want a little belt of cider?"

It took us a while to sort ourselves out. We ended up around the kitchen table, five of us now. Rusty took in all the calendars on the walls and the Clorox-bottle ivy planters.

"Really Middle America," she said to me in a semiwhisper.

But she eased in. She sat there like a big, bright

sunflower with her elbows on the table and the
bracelets crawling down her arms, telling us all about
California. We heard about this big wave they have at
Newport Beach called The Wedge, which is the surfer's ultimate test, and how she happened to end up
here, in Middle America.

"My mom's an FA," Rusty said.

"A what?" Polly was missing nothing.

"Flight attendant, and my dad's a pilot for the
same airline. They were transferred out here as a
package deal, and we've got a condo in The Meadows
of Greenbriar. With overtime, my dad's pulling
down some nice money, but of course he's got kids
from his first couple of marriages to pay for."

"Do tell," said Polly Prior, and Rusty did.

All this time Kate was tracing little designs on the
tabletop with the side of her thumb, listening, and
wondering what I was up to. It was pretty clear that
her Homecoming plans didn't include anybody extra. Her eyes kept studying Rusty, but her mind was
way off somewhere on another topic.

We got to talking about school things. Trav brought
up the subject. "What are California schools like?"

Rusty leaned back in the chair. "Basically op-
tional," she said. "You've got your burnouts and your
Vals and your heads and your modified heads and
your granola people. You've got your Souls, your An-
glos, your low-riders, your boat people. Everybody's
in little boxes." She paused. "Like here, come to
think about it, but the climate's better."

"I meant academically," Trav said.

Rusty thought about that—thought about Trav, maybe.

"It's there if you want it, but most people are majoring in personal image. Basically, it's too easy. Even with a room-temperature IQ you can pull down a couple of *A*'s for the report card. That's enough to mellow out most parents. So then you think, Why worry?"

"Like here," Trav said. "Like everywhere."

"And teachers?" Kate said, coming into this.

"The teachers are burning out faster than we are," Rusty said. "Of course, they've got to hustle harder than we do, but then, it's their job, right?"

Kate was listening now. "What do you think of Sherrie Slater?"

Rusty thought. Her finger traced the wet ring her cider glass left on the table. "I feel sorry for her."

Kate looked at Rusty like they'd just met that minute. I had the vague idea the sides weren't evening up exactly like I'd meant.

Finally, I got a word in. "The thing is," I said to Polly, "Rusty's going to Homecoming with us, so she needs a costume too."

Kate turned wide gray eyes upon me.

Polly turned her little pink ones on Rusty. Rusty was sitting there in her own layered look. A couple of layers looked like fish netting, and the top one was a loose, sleeveless item made out of a gunnysack with a ripped neck. A matching sweatband held back her red curls. She had peacock-blue stuff shading her eyelids and brown lipstick, and in her ears all eight earrings. One of them looked a lot like a safety pin.

"Ain't that a costume right there?" asked Polly, genuinely stumped.

We skipped the game. Kate's plan was to meet in the evening at the bonfire. There was a nip in the air, and my new furry body felt good. The gorilla head was a nice fit too. I edged out of the trailer and started lumbering over to the MacDowells' back steps, where Irene and Scotty and Dad were sitting out. I hunched over, letting my arms swing, as I came down Irene's garden rows in the moonlight. I had this plan to scare the wits out of them—at least Irene.

She looked up and saw me. "Hi, Buck," she said.

Scotty said to Dad, "That boy is getting to favor you more and more in looks. I hope he's got better sense, though."

"Don't put your money on it," Dad remarked, so I lumbered off down the road.

The bonfire drew quite a crowd, and beyond it the lights were beginning to strobe in the gym for the dance. Dark figures moved in front of the crackling orange flames.

Most of the costumes were on the freshmen: a few Smurfs and pointy-earred gremlins, some intergalactic types. Nothing noticeably historical. The sophomores made token efforts: a lot of dark glasses and single rhinestoned gloves. The uncostumed juniors and seniors had pulled their cars up close and were lounging on fenders and swigging unidentified liquids out of paper sacks.

It was a good bonfire, whooshing up, even getting little rounds of applause from the fender people. Then, outlined in orange, I saw the shape of Trav's Army hat. He looked great, really authentic. I wasn't hard for him to spot. In fact, I was getting quite a lot of attention.

"You're looking good," Trav said, bending over and peering into my eye holes. "But I don't quite see what Slocum Township historical period you represent."

*Pre*historical," I said. "Not many costumes around, though. The juniors and seniors are trying to rise above it."

"Who cares?" Trav said. "Who's in a hurry to be like them?" He seemed to be somebody else in his uniform. In the stiff collar he looked relaxed. His dad, Mr. Kirby, was there in his role as president of the school board, but Trav was keeping the bonfire between them.

We spotted Kate. She was there with Rusty, and you couldn't miss either one of them. Rusty either was or wasn't in costume: a short-skirted, strapless formal dress from maybe the fifties worn over a body stocking in camouflage colors. She looked like a flash-dancing urban guerrilla, and this was her own creation, nothing from Polly's past. Her sneakers appeared to be of two different colors.

In Polly's graduation dress, Kate didn't even look like she was in costume. She wore a shawl with fringe draped around her shoulders, and she carried a fan. People kept stopping to look at her. Nobody could have pulled this off but Kate. When Trav and I came up, she and Rusty looked thick as thieves.

We watched the bonfire burn down. Trav and I did. Kate was checking out the crowd. The music started thumping in the gym, and people began wandering over there. Kate and Rusty were walking along ahead of us. I noticed when Rusty nudged Kate. The plot was definitely thickening.

"We're not going to the dance," Kate said over her shoulder. "We're going . . . someplace else, back toward my house. You guys stay with Rusty. Keep behind me, way back. No matter what, just keep your distance."

Rusty dropped back with Trav and me. "She's got a plan," she said, pursing her blueberry-colored lips.

Kate walked away from us. In the shadow behind the propped-open gym door a big figure was hunched against the wall, smoking. His jacket collar was pulled up, and a John Deere cap was riding low on his head. When he took a drag on the cigarette, it lit up his face. Skeeter. Kate was stepping up to him.

"Wait a minute," I said, but Rusty was between Trav and me, grabbing our arms and leading us into the gym.

I just managed to hear Kate say, "Got another cigarette on you, Skeet? I'm dying for one." I saw his squint when he looked up at her through the smoke, and then his eyes widened.

"Hold it. For one thing, she doesn't smoke," I said,

but we were already in the gym, and Rusty about had me in a hammerlock.

"I don't like this," Trav said.

"It gets better," said Rusty.

We stood there while people surged in around us. A few people felt my fur.

"This makes no sense, Rusty," I said. "Skeeter's a maniac. We got to get out there and—"

"Give her time," Rusty said. "She's got this worked out like—"

"D-Day," Trav said.

"Right." Rusty nodded. "So don't blow it."

It seemed about an hour, but it wasn't. Finally we started back outside against the flow of people. They were coming in like cattle through a hedge. But nobody was out there behind the door. Just shadows.

I think Trav panicked. I think I did. But Rusty pointed off past the bonfire toward the road. You could see Kate's skirts and this lumpy shape beside her: Skeeter's. They were moving fast into the dark together. I considered taking out after them to give Skeeter another opportunity to beat me to death. Trav turned his hands up in the air. "Why is this happening?"

"Keep with them, but keep back," Rusty said, heading out.

It was pitch dark on the road. You could see where you were going, but that was about it. I was trying to move fast, and I was steaming up inside my gorilla head. I never thought about taking it off. But Rusty was setting the pace, holding us back. You could hear

the silky sound of her formal dress over her body
stocking. If I'd known she was as bossy as Kate, I'd
have thought twice about inviting her in the first
place.

We were halfway to Kate's house when a car pulled
out of a lane behind us, throwing gravel. When the
headlights beamed down the road, you could see
Kate and Skeeter. They were ambling along, taking
their time. I wondered what she was saying to him. I
wondered what he was thinking. He probably
couldn't believe his luck. The car shot past us. Then
the brakes squealed, and the brake lights showed red
all over the blacktop.

It looked like the car stopped a few yards ahead of
Kate and Skeeter. The door on the driver's side
banged open, and the taillights flickered as somebody moved around the back bumper.

"Bingo," said Rusty.

I'd had about enough of this, and so had Trav. He
lit out, and I did my best in my flapping coat. Rusty
kept up with us.

I couldn't see much except the taillights through a
fog from the exhaust. Then the light color of Kate's
dress. She was standing at the edge of the blacktop,
looking down in the ditch. It was like running in a
dream. It took forever. When we came up to her, we
could see two shapes in the ditch, and Skeeter wasn't
on top.

An enormous guy in a warm-up jacket was all over
him. You could see his fists flailing, pale and oversize,
pounding in a rhythm. The sound was incredible, like

TV. He was pounding Skeeter's face into ground round. Skeeter was helpless, and it went on and on.

"No," Trav said when he saw. "This isn't the way."

The guy was crouched over Skeeter, and Skeet's legs were kicking out, slower and slower.

The guy stood up then. Even down in the ditch he was eye to eye with us. A really big guy, an adult, with a crew cut. I'd never seen him before in my life.

He worked his hands together. He couldn't have had much skin left on his knuckles. Then he looked down at Skeeter, who was writhing around. I couldn't see Skeet's face, but he wasn't having a good night. The big guy made a sideways move, kicked Skeeter in the side of the head, and climbed out of the ditch.

"You kids need a ride?" He was breathing heavy.

"We're practically home," Kate said, quiet, calm.

Skeet was moaning, thrashing around. The car pulled away, and it was really dark. Eerie.

"We can't leave him there," Trav said. "He may need help."

"Then let him crawl out and get it," Kate said. She was walking off down the road, fiddling with her fan. She was this elegant young lady out for an evening stroll. We fell in with her.

"I told you I'd get him," she said, "even if it took me a while. I said I'd find a way."

"But not like this," Trav said. "Skeeter's a disturbed kid. He's troubled."

"I don't care if he's troubled," Kate said. "He's *trouble*. He was getting worse, and nobody was doing anything. Everybody was trying to live around him. Nobody's in charge here. Skeeter counted on that. I had to find somebody who wasn't about to take it."

"Who was it?" Trav said. "Who was the guy in the car?"

"Mr. Slater."

Mr. Slater? I couldn't believe it. "You mean Sherrie Slater's husband? She has a husband?"

"What did you think that ring on her finger was for? I saw them one night, shopping over at Southgate Mall. He didn't look like the type who'd put up with somebody hassling his wife. I looked them up in the south suburban phone book. I called up and kept calling till he answered. Then I just told him what was going on. I told him who'd stolen his wife's car and about the Xeroxed hands. I told him a lot and he bought it. It was true."

"Legally it wasn't," Trav said. "You convicted Skeeter on circumstantial evidence."

"It took all last spring for the circumstantial evidence to heal up on my head," I said, just for the record. Personally, I was pretty impressed with Kate's brand of justice. It got down to basics.

"It was true," Kate said.

"You set Skeeter up," I said.

She nodded. "We made a plan. I worked out some of it. Mr. Slater worked out the rest."

We'd come to the lane of her house. "Listen, you'd better not come in tonight. Polly would smell a rat right away. I don't want her knowing about this. Why should she? It's taken care of. So I'll see all you guys later, okay?" She turned, gathering up her skirts. We just stood there in our various disguises, watching her go.

"Far out," Rusty breathed.

Trav had his uniform hat off and was raking his hand through his hair. "It's wrong, and Kate can't see it. There isn't a simple solution to everything. There's no simple solution to anything."

He saw a link between himself and Skeeter. It seemed pretty farfetched to me, but it was there.

"Let me get this straight," I said to him. "When Skeet pounds on me, he's a troubled kid. But when Mr. Slater pounds on Skeet, it's what? Assault and battery?"

"Yes," Trav said, "and we're accessories."

"Really far out," Rusty murmured.

"Come on," Trav said. "We've got to go back and see if we can do anything for him."

The wind came up, winterish. It'd be pretty damp in that ditch, as I had reason to know. Rusty hesitated, but then she said, "Maybe we better."

We found the place back up the road, but Skeeter was gone. We made sure.

"Climbed out and limped home," I said.

Trav stood there in the road, slapping the hat against his leg, really frustrated. "See? What did this solve? It didn't solve anything. And it didn't take Kate long to forget how much she hates violence. Why can't I get her to understand? Why can't I make people hear me?"

It was cold out there, and I was getting clammy

inside my fur skin. "I'm hearing you, Trav," I said. "And Rusty. We're hearing you."

I couldn't see his eyes in the dark. I didn't know what he was seeing until he spoke again. "It could just as well have been me in that ditch instead of Skeeter."

"No it couldn't. You wouldn't—"

"Skeeter acts out all his aggressions, and I just keep mine in and let them eat at me. That's not much of a difference."

"I guess Kate just figures that Skeeter's a danger to the public. . . ." I didn't finish the thought. I didn't get around to the one person Trav was a danger to. I guess I couldn't because that person was standing right there with Rusty and me.

"What did this solve?" he said again, looking down at the black ditch. "It didn't solve anything."

But it seemed to. Skeeter dropped out of school. I guess he wasn't about to turn up with a crusty face and a new nose. He was probably of legal age to quit anyhow. A minor rumor went around that he'd joined the Army, but nobody was too interested after the first relief. I personally thought we could get along without Skeeter, but it bothered Trav. What didn't?

Sherrie Slater dropped out too. She resigned at the end of the first semester. She didn't announce it in class, but we knew. She'd taken Kate aside and told her she was quitting, that she was pregnant.

Kate said she looked really happy—and relieved. I

asked her if Sherrie had known about what happened on Homecoming night.

"She did and she didn't," Kate said. "Adults aren't that different from us. They know just about what they want to know."

CHAPTER ELEVEN

By the spring of the year, both Kate and Trav were beginning to make their marks around school. They were getting noticed for the right things by the right people. They were showing evidence of developing into a couple of stars. Two out of three ain't bad.

Trav ended up the first semester with a perfect grade-point average, all *A*'s, the only one in the class. They ran his picture in the *Slocum Township Topics* and a piece about him in the school newspaper headlined FRESHMAN T. KIRBY RAISES CLASS AVERAGE SINGLE-HANDEDLY. A lot of people were impressed, though Trav wasn't one of them. As a reward, his folks wanted to take him someplace, to Sanibel Island for the semester break, but he talked them out of it.

In the second semester he joined the debate team, and it didn't take him long to become their main man, even as a freshman. This was something he could really get his teeth into. These debaters were very big on major international issues. They played chess just to unwind, and they didn't play Trivial

Pursuit because it was too trivial. Trav was meeting new people, becoming known. He was looking good.

Needless to say, so was Kate. Ever since Homecoming, a lot of the older guys had begun discovering her. They started hanging out at her locker. You about had to take a number to get near her.

"Who are all these guys, anyway?" I'd say to her in the midst of her throng.

"What guys?" She'd look around, very innocent.

There were too many of them, and some of them were enormous, so I lived through my jealous phase. Maybe I didn't mind so much as long as it wasn't Trav.

Rusty Hazenfield would skate past, making her usual lightning raids. For spring she was heavy into an ethnic look: beaded headache band, feather barrettes, a loosely laced-up leather vest top—part Grace Jones, part Pocahontas.

"Just one, Kate," she'd sing out, swinging past, putting up one green-nailed finger. "Spare just one for me. You can't handle them all."

Then she'd give big eyes to all the guys—babes—and move off. Down the hall she'd go, snapping her fingers to her own beat and singing a snatch from "Girls Just Want to Have Fun."

And me? I kept busy. From the day I turned fifteen, the learner's permit was burning a hole in my pocket. We all got them, but mine meant more to me. As my first long-term goal, I was making plans for a car of my own, at least by senior year. Scotty said he'd take me on at the Sunoco in the summer. I'd spent

Christmas up in Cleveland to see Mom and to get her to understand I wanted a summer here, not there.

I was already making some extra money from Irene and Scotty. They were rebuilding the garage of the Sunoco as a convenience store, kind of a home-grown 7-Eleven. I'd picked up enough carpentry from being around Dad to make myself useful, fitting wallboard.

Scotty was a master mechanic, but the whole neighborhood was turning into import territory, and people were taking their cars back to the dealerships for maintenance. These places said they had Euro-pean-trained mechanics whether they did or not, so Scotty was hurting for business.

A convenience store with a few grocery staples and impulse items seemed the only way, though Irene was more hopeful about it than Scotty was. Dad and I helped them out in the evenings. Dad wouldn't take any money from Scotty, but Irene brought down supper for us. Scotty didn't do much strummin' anymore, but we had some good times. It was family.

Kate and Trav and I were moving out in these different directions. It was getting harder to keep in touch, and we weren't as tight as before. Maybe we'd been too tight, but I missed the way we'd been.

I must have been in this nostalgic mood one day between classes when Rusty materialized again.

"Hey, Rusty," I said, "we ought to get together again one of these days, the four of us."

She smiled a dazzling smile. "What have you people got planned this time, an *assassination?*"

Somehow I'm never ready for Rusty. "No, I just meant—"

"You're not into another one of your jealousy trips about Kate and Trav, are you?" Large hazel eyes examined me.

I'm really never ready for Rusty. "If you mean last fall, that wasn't exactly why I—"

"Sure it was." Rusty nodded. "But look, I didn't mind. It was a hoot. Oh, I don't just mean the part about Mr. Slater playing hit man for Kate. That real old lady was interesting too. I mean, cider out of a jug? It was right out of *Little House on the Prairie,* you know? Sure, we can get together again sometime. Maybe. But you know what? I got funny vibes around the three of you. I mean, I liked you fine, but I got vibes."

Vibes? "We sort of grew up together."

Rusty hitched up her book bag. "Well, keep it up. You know what I mean?"

Not exactly, but she was gone. There's more to Rusty than meets the eye.

"Meet me in the auditorium in about ten minutes," Kate said, whisking past one day after school. She was practically moving at Rusty's rate of speed, and she definitely had something in mind.

"Trav too?"

"If you can find him. I need all the moral support I can get."

Somehow I didn't find him.

The only lights in the auditorium were on the bare stage. I thought the place was empty, but then I saw Kate hunched in a seat on the back row, shadowed by the balcony. I walked along the row to her.

"Just sit down and hold my hand," she said.

Anything to oblige. Her hand was like ice, and now she wasn't talking. A couple of teachers I didn't know came onto the stage from the wings and began fiddling with the mike and the lights.

"Mrs. Pratt," Kate murmured, meaning the white-haired woman, "and Mr. Handelsman. They're the speech and drama department."

Not one of my electives, but I'd seen Mr. Handelsman around. He always wore a tweed jacket with elbow patches over jeans. By then girls were filtering into the dark auditorium. Some of them were slipping in through the emergency exits.

"Spring play," Kate murmured. "Tryouts for the female roles, and there are only two of them." She was checking out the other girls. "Only two parts, I mean."

Kate's cold hand told the rest of the story. She was trying out.

"Why am I doing this? They'll give both parts to seniors. I don't have a prayer."

There were quite a few senior-looking girls settling into the front seats, trying to create space around themselves. Most of them were reasonably foxy.

"Bimbos," I remarked. "You're a shoo-in."

"Don't even speak." She had my hand in a death

grip. "I'm either going to start crying or throw up."
She didn't mention leaving.

Mr. Handelsman walked over to the mike and
started laying out some ground rules. The play was to
be *The Glass Menagerie* by Tennessee Williams. He
said it was a "memory play" that they were going to
do, with only a suggestion of costuming and stage
sets. "It will be mainly a matter of lighting and your
own skills in evoking the characters."

Kate slipped lower in her seat.

Mr. Handelsman said they weren't going to read
parts from the play today. Any girl trying out was to
give something else she'd worked up. She could use
the mike or not, whichever she wanted, and since
there were a lot of people here, who wanted to be
first?

Knowing Kate, I figured she'd be up on the stage in
a flash to be first and get it over with. Do I know
Kate? She was sinking so low in the seat, I nearly lost
her. Other girls started up on the stage, some cool,
some forcing themselves.

They did all kinds of stuff. One of them stood on a
ladder and did something from *Our Town*. One was
Shakespeare's Juliet, followed by one who did a Joan
Rivers impression. One of them looked like Linda
Ronstadt and really knew it. We had everything up
there but baton twirlers. Some were bad, and some I
had to admit were excellent. When somebody was
especially good, or looking good, Kate would
whisper, "One more like that and I leave."

Sometime after five o'clock she jerked her hand

away, stood up, and headed down the aisle. A long
trip. Around then I began to wonder what she was
going to do when she got up on the stage. The rest of
them had their material down cold, whatever it was.
Kate climbed the stage steps, gave her name to Mrs.
Pratt, looked at the mike, and walked away from it.

She came down to the edge of the stage. I don't
remember what she was wearing. You didn't usually
notice. The lights above lightened her hair. It was
smooth, propped behind her ears. She seemed to
know exactly where to stand. She looked down at the
auditorium like it was full. When she looked up again,
the lights touched her face. Then she began to speak.
It was a poem, just eight lines. No gestures, no moving around. You could hear her, too, every word ring-
ing just right:

> "The days of winter enter in,
>   The darkness nibbles at the days,
>   The heavy clouds pull down the sky,
>   The first deep snowfall stays, and grays.
>
> "Too long to wait for springtime now
>   Here in this cold and darkening room,
>   Only time for remembering
>   The pear trees all in bloom."

That was it. She didn't act it out, but you felt the
cold in the room and saw the snow change color. You
remembered pear trees blooming, and it really got to
you, even though she didn't let her voice break. It
was short and simple, but somehow you forgot about

Juliet and Joan Rivers and everybody else. The people left in the auditorium were quiet. Mrs. Pratt looked at Mr. Handelsman, and he looked back at her. Then Kate walked down the steps and let the auditorium swallow her up.

She got the part. They had to look at a lot more girls, and then everybody had to come back and read from the play. But Kate got the part of Laura, the lame girl in the play, and I personally think there was no question about it.

As far as I could see, Kate and Laura were nothing alike. Laura was this girl who lived in a dreamworld of little glass animals she collects in this steamy-hot apartment. She's really withdrawn and won't even go to school, while her mother looks for a boy to marry her, a Gentleman Caller, they call him. But Kate decided to be Laura, and she had till the end of May to make it work.

"So I want you guys at my place as often as possible, okay?" She meant Trav and me, and she meant business. She already had four copies of the play, and we were supposed to give her her lines.

She rehearsed with the cast every day, but she wanted an edge. So that was our spring, back together again. Trav had debate meetings and computer club, and Kate had to be at the real rehearsals, and I had my carpentry. But we worked it out in scraps of time. We were tighter than ever. We rehearsed at Kate's, and the fourth script was for Polly.

"We're exactly right," Kate said. "There are four of us, like the play. Buck, you're Tom, Laura's brother.

And Trav, you're the gentleman caller. And Polly, you're Amanda Wingfield, the mother."

"I can't see this little bitty print," Polly said, squinting. Also: "Whatever happened to cards? I didn't see hide nor hair of you kids all winter, and now we don't even get to have us a game. What kind of a woman is this Amanda Wingfield, anyhow?"

"She loves her children," Kate said, "and she drives them crazy."

"Typecasting," I remarked, and Polly shook her fist at me. Trav studied his part. You'd have thought we all four were going on the stage with it. We read and reread until we knew it without scripts, except for my longer speeches, which we left out. They were a little too poetic for me.

We had that play down cold, and I was wishing it was an assignment for English, but after Sherrie Slater left, we had a string of substitutes, so we weren't doing much of anything in English.

There was a scene in *The Glass Menagerie* when the gentleman caller kisses Laura, but Trav and Kate skimmed past that. A senior guy had gotten the part of the gentleman caller, and Kate said she'd save her kisses for him. I checked out Trav to see how he took that information. He took it calmly.

Polly learned her part first, even before Kate, except she kept wanting to change it. I think she studied it during the day when we were at school.

"That Amanda Wingfield is nuttier than a fruitcake. I wouldn't have said any of that stuff. And she's always carrying on about how many boyfriends she had when she was a girl. She simpers, and she talks too much."

Trav looked up from his script at Polly. He was wearing horn-rims by then. He and Polly were lens to lens. "I bet you had a lot of boyfriends when you were a girl." It was a very mellow thing for Trav to say.

Polly looked away, and her hand crept up to the knot of hair on her neck. "A couple," she said. "Three or four."

Kate watched her. Kate was all business and kept us on track, but she gave Polly time to remember. "Where were we?" Polly said, bringing her script up to her nose.

When the weather warmed up, we took our show out on the porch. That worked pretty well, too, because some of the play takes place out on a fire escape. Laura in the play is somewhat lame, but she thinks she's a cripple. Kate practiced Laura's moves up and down the porch floor past the cream separator, learning the limp, learning not to overuse it.

She didn't go show biz on us. She was never satisfied with her performance, and she never forgot us, even when she didn't need us as much to cue her.

"You people are better than the real cast," she'd say, and we always agreed.

Sometimes she wanted Trav and me out in the yard so she could pitch her voice across space. You'd think hearing the same lines over and over would get monotonous, but it didn't. One time Trav and I were stretched out in the grass, being audience, and I said to him, "She's an actress, isn't she? I mean, a real one." I figured he'd know.

He was propped up on his elbows, relaxed in the grass. "Yes. She believes in herself, and so you believe in her too. We always have."

I maybe understood that. "Someday we'll be able to say we knew her when."

"You will." Trav's eyes were on Kate in the distance. "I won't be here."

I thought he meant he'd be out in the world, being a success himself. Maybe at Harvard or someplace like that. I don't know what I thought.

"I knew her first," I said, sort of kidding.

That brought him around. His eyebrows rose above his horn-rims. "Didn't we all get together in eighth grade? I thought we did."

I remembered Kate and me watching the foal being born, the two of us as kids together, just the two of us. But the horse farm wasn't even there anymore. Now it was a half-built shopping mall, and I guessed it didn't matter.

"Come to think of it," I said, "it must have been eighth grade."

Kate knew she was ready, and I think they were amazed at her in the real rehearsals, though she never said. It was spring then, a warm one. Overnight the pear trees blossomed out. Polly sat on the porch, hearing Kate's lines, mouthing them silently herself while she faced the orchard, drinking it in.

One evening Trav and I were heading home down

the lane. You could smell all the spring smells mixing in, even lilac from somewhere. It reminded me of that poem, the one about remembering the pear trees in bloom. It sort of dawned on me.

"You wrote the poem Kate used at her tryout, didn't you?"

Trav was trudging along with twenty pounds of books under his arm, since we were coming up for finals. He shrugged.

"It was just a rough draft. Remember how Sherrie Slater always wanted us to write for ten minutes at the beginning of the period, and we never did?"

I remembered.

"When we found out she was quitting her job, I jotted it down one day in class—her last day. I left it on her desk."

I could picture him doing that, finding an indirect way of saying good-bye, letting Sherrie Slater know it hadn't been a complete loss. I wished I'd written something, too, though I didn't know what or how.

"You mean you wrote that poem in ten minutes?"

"With time left to make a copy for Kate." Trav dug me with his free elbow. "I budgeted my time."

Then at the end of the lane we went different ways.

I guess that was as tight as the three of us ever were. Trav writing a poem and Kate putting it to use and me finally figuring it out. That was the best time, the springtime, and I thought we had a lot to look forward to together.

CHAPTER TWELVE

We had big plans for the night of the play —Kate's plans, mostly. I don't remember every detail. It doesn't matter. Trav and I weren't supposed to be in the front row.

"You two know the play too well," she said. "You'd start prompting."

Kate's mom was going to be there if she got around to it, and we'd asked Polly if she wanted to go. We could work her wheelchair into the side of the auditorium. But she said she'd stay home. She said she didn't want to see anybody doing it but us. There was a lot of talk about the play around school. It was going to be a full house.

Dad and I were working over at Irene and Scotty's that evening. I figured I could work awhile before I had to get cleaned up and ready to go. I remember Dad and Scotty and I were laying the Formica top on the checkout counter. I remember we had this long, involved discussion about what to call Irene and Scotty's store. Finally we decided to call it Irene and Scotty's Store and thought it was a dynamite name.

Then the pay phone rang out in the station. "You want to get that, Buck?" Irene said. She was up on a ladder, fitting shelves. So I went out and picked up.

"I only have one call." It was Trav's voice, sounding far off, tinny.

"What's happening?"

"Can you come down here? I can only make this one call." His voice had an edge on it, and I wasn't hearing enough.

"Where are you?"

"Police station. The one in Southwood."

Police station? A joke?

"Can you come, Buck? Pretty soon? And bring your dad if you can." Then he hung up, and I was looking down in the receiver at the dial tone.

"I don't know what this means," I kept saying. "What's this supposed to mean?"

But Dad had dropped everything, and we were heading around back to the truck. He was digging in his pocket for the keys. We gunned out onto the route, and I had to be dazed, because I didn't even ask to drive.

"It could maybe be a joke."

"We'll laugh later," Dad said, flipping down the visor and working through the tail end of the rush-hour traffic.

Southwood's a couple of miles up the route from us. We pulled up in front of the police station and were climbing down out of the truck, and there wasn't anything particularly real about any of this.

"Is a boy here named Trav Kirby?" Dad said to the cop behind the counter. He glanced down at a clipboard and buzzed us in through a woven-wire door. All I could think of was *Hill Street Blues,* and then we saw Trav sitting in a chair along a cinder-block wall. No joke. His face was the same gray as the wall.

He looked too old to be himself, or too young. He was sitting like Polly sits sometimes in her wheel-chair, worn out but holding on. Then when he saw us, he looked away like a kid. It was ridiculous. It wasn't even happening.

Dad walked over and put his hand on Trav's shoulder. He was still wearing his school clothes, but he looked shrunken in them. When he felt Dad's hand, his eyes closed, and his head dropped back against the wall.

Another cop came in: the chief. "You've come about this boy?"

Dad nodded, and the chief looked him over, saw the sawdust on his arms and a claw hammer still hanging from a loop on Dad's pants. The chief looked a little relieved.

"What's the problem?" Dad said, keeping his hand on Trav.

"We have a complaint on him lodged by a merchant over at Southgate Mall. Discount house over there." He had on a gray uniform shirt with a badge and hash marks. Quite a bit of gray in his hair, like somebody cast for the part. Quiet, though, almost apologetic, not even armed. "Concealment of Merchandise is the charge, probably an A misdemeanor."

"Meaning?" Dad said.

"Merchandise valued at over fifty dollars, not to exceed four hundred and ninety-nine, ninety-nine. Shoplifting."

"What was it?"

"Well, it doesn't add up," the chief said. "Kids' things. Little kids'. Some toy cars, a G.I. Joe doll, one or two of them model kits to make a toy airplane, a plastic dinosaur. Such stuff as that—kind of a random sampling." The chief looked up. "Does he have a younger brother in the family?"

Dad shook his head, maintained eye contact. The chief looked uncomfortable. He started to put his hands on his hips, but then he rubbed his jaw instead.

"Possibility of a mistake?" Dad said. He and the chief weren't squaring off. They were working together, trying to.

"Looks pretty clear-cut."

Trav glanced up and started to say, "I—"

"Wait." Dad's hand tightened on Trav's shoulder.

The chief's hand was still cupping his chin. "How old is the boy?"

"Fifteen," Dad said, "the same as my son." He nodded to me.

The chief made a little move. "You mean this isn't your son?" He pointed right down in Trav's face.

"No," Dad said. "We're his friends."

Trav started to crumple then, but held on.

The chief was rubbing the back of his neck under his collar. "Does he have a father?"

Dad nodded.

"Then we've got to get him over here, don't we?"

"Yes," Trav said. "I guess we do."

It took Mr. Kirby quite a while to get there. He'd been tied up in rush-hour traffic. I had time to think but couldn't. I remember him coming into this windowless space where we were. He was in a three-piece suit, looking like he always did, like Trav thirty years later. Dad's hand slipped away and he stood back.

"Son, are you all right?" Mr. Kirby said. Trav sat a little straighter in the chair, bracing himself.

"Has there been an accident?" Mr. Kirby was looking around, and his eyes were lost. "Are there injuries?"

"Let me get this nailed down," the Chief said. "You're the father of this boy, yes or no?" And then he told him what he'd told us. We went through the whole thing again. I don't know how Mr. Kirby took it. I couldn't look to see.

It was quiet for a long time, and then he said, "Officer, I'm a lawyer."

The Chief made a little gesture. I guess it meant that Trav would need one.

"Will you release the boy in my custody?"

"The probation officer has the right to file a petition," the Chief said. "It can end in a court date, or the officer can handle the case informally."

"Yes," Mr. Kirby said, very quiet. "I'm familiar with the procedure."

The Chief rubbed the back of his neck again. It didn't seem to be any easier for him than for the rest of us. I halfway noticed how far all this was happening from Trav.

"There's a new civil penalty," the Chief said, "a separate action whereby the merchant can penalize. It involves repayment of the dollar value and an additional fine. It's an option."

"Yes," Mr. Kirby said, "I'm aware of that too."

There were papers to sign then. It got official, meaningless.

I thought Dad and I ought to go. I thought we ought to be someplace else, just about anyplace. But Dad was waiting for Mr. Kirby to finish up what he had to do and come over to Trav, to claim him. Dad wasn't going anywhere till then.

When Mr. Kirby turned away from the Chief's desk and came over to Trav, I thought he was going to help him stand, still playing this like an accident with injuries. Trav didn't move.

"Son, did you call Buck and Mr. Mendenhall when you couldn't get me?"

Trav looked up and spoke, almost in his own voice. "No, I called them first."

Mr. Kirby took that, but it hurt. When he could, he turned to Dad and said, "I thank you. We're grateful for our friends." He turned around, including me in. I saw his eyes were wet. He was a grown man, and it shook me.

We got out then, Dad and I first. If there was anything I could say to Trav, I don't know what it was, and this was definitely not the place. When we were outside, it was almost dark. I couldn't believe it. I thought time had been standing still. Kate's play was half over by now.

The Kirbys' BMW was parked out there, and Mrs. Kirby was in it. She didn't look up. She was just staring at the dashboard.

We swung up into the truck. Dad wedged himself behind the steering wheel, flipped up the visor. I thought we were moving out. But when he'd stuck the key into the ignition, he didn't turn loose of it.

Looking straight out the windshield, he said, "Whatever. Whenever. Call me first."

Then we moved out.

That next morning was picture-perfect, what all Saturdays should be. Big puffy clouds in a blue sky, a breeze moving in the pear trees. Polly's kitchen was like a cool cave, and Polly was there in her chair, waiting for the day to get going.

"Hoo-boy, you're in hot water," she said as soon as I loomed up at the screen door. "Katie's madder than hops that you two didn't turn out for the play." Her old hand worked over her mouth. "Worried too. You all right?"

I held up my arms to show her how I was, but before she could read anything in my face, Kate breezed in.

"Have that excuse ready, and make it good," she

said, very snappy, slanting past me to the refrigerator. "Why can't I ever keep any orange juice in here?" she said inside the refrigerator door. "Why are we always out?"

Polly was looking at me, both moons taking me in. "How bad is your news, Buck?" she said.

"Not good," I said, and Kate looked back and saw me.

"Go on out," Polly said. "The two of you, go on down to the orchard together." She made a quarter turn in her chair and looked away.

We walked down through the trees. Kate was putting off hearing. "For heaven's sake, even my mother managed to be there. She practically stood up and took a bow on my behalf. Everybody was there. They were standing along the walls."

"A hit?"

She nodded. "Where were you?" So then I had to tell her.

She let me finish—barely. She held herself back till then, pulling it all out of me with her eyes, not wanting to believe but believing. We were down in the little clearing, which was a mass of blossoms and blue sky.

"What are we doing down here?" Kate looked around like we'd made a wrong turn.

"Because we don't have anywhere else to be. None of this makes any sense. Trav didn't need those things he took."

Kate looked away, miles away. "Buck, do you remember the time he showed us his room? All those toys he'd kept. I never will forget it. There on his desk was an electric typewriter and all those books and papers—files, even. But up above, looking down, was every toy he'd been able to hold on to."

I remembered. "Then why did he need to . . . get any more?"

"He must have needed something else. To be caught. He had to know he'd be caught, and he was. He set himself up."

"Did he do it to . . . get back at his parents?" I said. "It was rough for his dad, rougher than I told you."

Kate lifted her shoulders. "If he did, I bet it was only because they're part of him. I think he was getting back at himself. Trav's a big burden for Trav to carry around all on his own. I think he just wanted to shift the burden, to stop having to be responsible."

"Why is Trav a bigger burden to himself than anybody else? Than us?"

The sun cleared the treetops and touched Kate. "I don't know." And then because she never likes not knowing, she said again, "What are we doing here? Why aren't we there with him now? Why do we keep letting him down?" She made a turn, and the wet grass tangled her feet.

"I don't know if I'd want to see us."

Kate shook her head. Her hair thrashed around. "Come on. We're wasting time." She went on ahead of me up the orchard, long strides, and I stepped where she stepped.

Up in the Kirbys' neighborhood, people were out

pruning and grooming their golf-green lawns. They were putting in begonias to border their driveways. They were riding these little toy tractors to make neat shapes in the mown grass. There's no high grass or tall trees up there at the top of Loire Drive, not even any shadows.

Half of the double doors opened before we could ring the bell at Trav's house. Mrs. Kirby opened the door, wearing a long thing like a robe, but her hair was tidy and shaped. She put out her hand to draw us in. "I didn't want to call. I just hoped you'd come."

We stood inside, and Mr. Kirby appeared, dressed for a regular Saturday morning. If you just glanced at them, they were normal.

"Trav's still upstairs," he said, forgetting to say hello. "We don't want to lean on him. We just want to work through this. I'm going to run up and tell him you're both here."

He nodded at us separately. "That's going to be a big help." He went up the stairs, two at a time.

"Is it going to be a warm day?" Mrs. Kirby said. "I thought we might take a drive just to get out of the house. I thought we might take a picnic and go somewhere. We could all go."

Kate pulled back from that, but Mrs. Kirby didn't notice. She turned, looking around the hall like Kate had looked around at the orchard. I couldn't think of anything to say. It was the police station all over again. I was just there, taking up space. I tried not to look up the stairs, even when somebody was coming down them.

It was Mr. Kirby. He stopped short on the bottom step. "Well, he's upset," he said. "He's been pushing himself too hard, and something had to give. He has a long history of it, doesn't he? He's been under a lot of pressure. This whole thing is just a way to . . . blow off steam. It's just an . . . episode. In a way, I think we ought to be glad."

"Yes," Mrs. Kirby said, "really, we should. We blame ourselves for not seeing, but you know how . . ." She looked at us and saw we were just kids, at least in her eyes.

Mr. Kirby hadn't moved. He was still standing on the bottom step, almost at attention—Trav's posture.

"I'm sorry," he said. "I'm sorry as I can be, but Trav doesn't want to see you right now. It's a little too soon. He's . . . confused. We're going to find some place for him where he can get some rest."

I could feel Kate's eyes on me. I'd said Trav wouldn't want to see us, and she was blaming me a little for knowing. What were we supposed to do, dodge past his parents, swarm up the stairs like a SWAT team, break down Trav's door, and be there for him?

Yes, Kate said later. Why not? What did we have to lose?

"We're so grateful to you both for coming and showing your concern," Mrs. Kirby was saying. She said the same thing again as we were going out the door.

But we couldn't just walk away. I looked back. "We won't say anything about this, Mrs. Kirby."

.I thought she might want to hear that, but she said, "It doesn't matter." She almost smiled in a ghostly way. "It will be on the . . . public record."

When we were out in the sunshine, the day was so normal, you wanted to blow it up sky-high.

"Listen," I said to Kate, loud in her ear, "we're just kids. That's all we are."

Then I grabbed her hand and started running flat out. She kept up with me because she had to. We ran down the perfect curve of Loire Drive. We pounded out of there.

That next week was finals, but Trav wasn't there for them. We had nobody to raise our class average single-handedly, but I don't think anybody particularly noticed. After all, summer's in sight, and it's what we're thinking about, what we've been living for.

"I think it's just as well," Kate said. "Trav's always so hyper about finals. He overdoes. He does too well. Let him find out he can live without them. It won't hurt him to miss once, will it?"

But I didn't know.

When the *Slocum Township Topics* came out that week, they ran a whole page of pictures from the play, and Kate was in every shot. She was the only one I saw. My brain blotted out the other people in the pictures, and I put Trav and Polly and me in their roles, our roles. I put us back together again.

CHAPTER THIRTEEN

Trav was gone all summer. It was a long hot one, and we didn't know where he'd been till he came back and told us. I pumped gas at the Sunoco while Irene and Scotty got their store going. I clocked more overtime than if I'd been legal working age.

Kate came down in the evenings to keep me company. The big old red vat full of pop was gone, but we were kept well supplied from the new refrigerated unit in the store. Kate and I sat out on the curb between customers, drinking pop. I wore official Sunoco coveralls, grease-soaked work shoes, and a ball cap.

"You smell like that time you went out for football," Kate said often.

"This here is the uniform of the honest working man."

"Give me a break," said Kate. Then we'd tussle somewhat and I'd threaten her seriously with the rag out of my back pocket that I used on dipsticks.

Once in a while she'd pitch in and squeegee a car

windshield while I was filling the tank. She'd scrub at splattered bugs like a wild woman, showing off for the customers. We'd be like a couple of little kids, except we were missing one of us. We talked around Trav. We waited.

I usually knocked off around nine o'clock, but I didn't shut down the pumps. Irene or Scotty would keep the store open. Between the two of them, they about kept it going twenty-four hours a day.

Kate was restless all that summer. One July night she said, "Quit early and come on up to see Polly. I'm worried about her. She's up to something, and I don't know what it is. She's got some notion."

"Where you two been?" Polly said when we got up there. "A person could dry up and blow away." She was in the kitchen, sitting in the dark, because the bugs were biting on the porch.

It was true I hadn't seen her in a while, and she was looking smaller in the chair. She could look extra pathetic, too, when she wanted to. Kate went around turning on lights.

"Seems like we don't have any fun anymore," Polly said, shifting around in her chair. She skewered me with one of her looks and fingered her chin, so I didn't know how serious to take her.

Kate rounded on her. "Now, Polly, you've got something on your mind. It's making you real cranky. What is it?"

Polly took her time. She straightened out her skirt over her knees, made little changes in the direction of her chair. She had on a big old pair of floppy bedroom slippers, and she leaned forward, examining them. We stood there, waiting her out.

"Well, it don't bear, does it?" she said. "You have to run an orchard like a business. You've got to spray, you've got to prune, you've got to harvest, or what's it for?"

Kate sighed.

"There isn't a reason in the world to keep it, is there?" Polly said. "Well, it's pretty in the spring of course, but then what? Besides, how many more springs have I got?"

"Lots," Kate said, loud. She reached out and gave the wheelchair arm a jerk, making Polly wobble. "You've got lots of springs left."

You're too mean to die, I wanted to say, but I couldn't get it out.

"So I've made up my mind," Polly said. "And you know what my mind's like when I've made it up. I'm going to sell off that orchard. I can get big money for it from one of them real estate developers."

Kate slapped her forehead, gave it a real crack. "So that's it. Well, you can just forget it, Polly. We can get along without selling off the orchard. We always have. They've practically paved the rest of Slocum Township, and they're not going to get your orchard. Has somebody been bugging you about this? Because if they have—"

"I made my own inquiries," Polly said, very dignified.

"Then they'll be all over you if they think you're willing to sell. And you know what'll happen: They'll bulldoze everything right up to the house. And they'll stick in as many houses as they can fit. They won't even have yards. They call it . . . What do they call it, Buck?"

"Cluster housing," I said.

"That's right," Kate said. "You'll have hundreds of people living on top of you, staring in your windows."

"I won't be here long to see it," Polly said.

Boy, that upset Kate. "Now stop that—"

"And neither will you, Katie," Polly said.

It got quiet then, very quick, while Kate thought about that.

"Oh, I'm beginning to see."

"Well, it's about time," Polly said, a little bit sniffy. "If I don't look to the future, I don't know who will."

"You mean that money for me, don't you, Polly?" Kate stood over her, close.

"I mean it for your education." Polly looked up at me, trying to remove Kate from this conversation. "A girl like that deserves the best education there is. Ain't that right, Buck?"

What could I say? "Yes."

Kate shot me a look. "I'll get an education, Polly. I'll get it somehow, and you don't have to worry about that."

"Well, I don't mean just any education. I mean the best one there is. I mean one of them real good colleges. I don't just know which one."

Kate reached out to Polly's hand, gripping the arm of the chair. "And don't jostle my chair," Polly said. "It makes me nervous."

Kate put both her hands up to the sides of her face, held it firm. "Oh, Polly," she said in almost a whisper, "what am I going to do with you?"

"Let me have my way," Polly said, just as quiet. "Let me do this for you, Katie." She looked around on the linoleum away from our eyes. "You don't know how bad I want it."

Then that whole kitchen got so blurry, I couldn't even see it.

It wasn't that night. It was another one soon after, hot as blazes. We had both air conditioners blasting in the trailer. I thought it was too hot to sleep, but I must have. Somewhere off in a dream I heard Dad running.

It woke me, and when I sat up, the trailer door was open and still swinging on its hinges. You could feel the night air outside, pushing in, muggy. I didn't have anything on but a pair of Jockey shorts, but I reached for my pants, which aren't ever too far away. Outdoors, I was still zipping them up, but I didn't see Dad. Somehow, I thought I ought to be running.

I took out around the Sunoco. The lights were still burning over the drive, and the pumps were on. But I didn't see anybody. There weren't even any cars going by on the route. When I looked out over the drive, I saw little pinpoints of silver. I couldn't make them out. Closer up, I saw it was change: nickels, dimes, quarters, a couple of fifty-cent pieces, all of it out there among the grease spots on the pavement.

I heard some sound behind me and whirled around

to the store. The front door was wedged partway open. It looked like a shoe jammed into the door, and then I saw it was someone lying there with his foot flung out, keeping the door from closing. A figure was bent over him, and over them both I saw Irene like a statue. I just saw these three in silhouette, because all the lights were on behind them in the store.

I moved closer, slow, in a dream. It was Scotty lying there with his foot in a work shoe, propping the door open, like he'd started outside and fallen back. And it was Dad crouching over him. Dad's shirt was off, like mine, and Scotty was lying slumped there against Dad's chest with his head fallen forward. There was blood, a lot of it, on the front of Scotty's shirt and smeared on Dad. When he looked up at me, he was the only one who moved. Scotty didn't, and neither did Irene. She stood over them in her bathrobe with the belt on it pulled tight enough to cut her in two.

"The police are on their way, with the paramedics," Dad said. "Get out in the road, Buck, and flag them in when you see them."

So I was out in the road, and now it was a nightmare. I didn't even need to be here. Dad just wanted me away from them. At first it made no sense to me, and then I saw the pattern pulling together.

It ran in my head like a tape, the way it had to have been. I could see a car pull up by the pumps and somebody—maybe a couple of them—checking out the store, seeing Scotty in there by himself, and the cash register. I saw them moving up on the door and going inside. Then the gun, and Scotty looking down the barrel of it and being told to scoop out the money drawer.

I saw them with the cash, backing to the door, leaving a silver trail. Then Scotty taking out after them, trying to get a make on their plates. Or just taking out after them. I seemed to hear the gunfire that Dad heard, even asleep, even over the whine of the air conditioner.

Then coming down the route were revolving blue lights, and you could hear the sirens way off.

The *Slocum Township Topics* ran a front-page piece on the mounting crime rate. I remember the headline:

GROWING SUBURBAN DISTRICT
VIRTUALLY LAWLESS
Senseless Shooting and Robbery of Convenience
Store Nets Eighty-five Dollars

and change.

This caused a big boom in the burglar-alarm business, and there was a lot of talk about how something ought to be done. The usual debate on handgun control broke out, and people took their usual sides.

Scotty lingered on for a week in the hospital. He'd taken two blasts in the chest from a Saturday-night special. The cops caught them later, the perpetrators. There were a couple of them, holding up a Wendy's north of the city. Then when they were out on bail, they were caught again holding up an all-night Stop & Shop.

Scotty was in an oxygen tent and hooked up to a machine. He never spoke or moved, but Dad took off from work and sat there with him every day. He and Irene spelled one another between the hospital and the store. I worked the business with one or the other of them. Dad didn't want me there by myself.

At the end of the week, Scotty died. Irene was at the hospital with him. When she came back, I was outside gassing up a car, and I knew what had happened by watching her walk over to the store. I thought about staying out by the pumps, but it seemed gutless.

Irene was standing by the counter when I came in behind her. I'd never noticed how much gray she had in her hair. She was wearing an old work shirt of Scotty's.

"It's all over," she said to Dad. He was coming toward her but stopped. She had her big old plastic purse in her hand. She slammed it down on the counter top, and you could hear things breaking inside it. "I don't know why I'm alive. I wish I was dead."

She stood there tall as a tree. She had shoulders on her like a man, and they were still straight, not slumped.

She looked at Dad. "I won't break down. I told myself I wouldn't." She gazed around at the store we'd built, all the shelves of canned goods and the potato-chip display rack and the piles of magazines. She'd had a lot of hope for the place.

"Besides, you lost him too," she said to Dad.

"I lost the best friend I ever had," he said, and his voice was thick in his throat. "I lost an arm off my body."

Irene's hand came up to her mouth, and she fought with herself. Dad put out his arms. "Cry with me, Irene. I can't do it alone." Then she stumbled against him.

CHAPTER FOURTEEN

It was Labor Day afternoon, and we were looking at sophomore year, a day away. For once I was about ready to go back to school. There'd been too many changes, and I thought some routine might help. Kate was more or less in the same frame of mind. For one thing, she wouldn't set foot in the orchard, wouldn't even look at it.

Polly had sold it, and the surveyor's little markers were already up. They'd cut a rough track from the county road in as far as Kate's clearing to start hauling out the trees and brush.

So we were sitting in the kitchen, playing three-handed rummy. The flypaper hanging down was crusted black, and it was hot enough to pop corn on the linoleum. But nobody wanted to sit out on the porch with a view of the orchard. It was sort of off limits in our minds.

Kate's mom was home that afternoon, but you didn't see much of her. She was upstairs blow-drying her hair.

"She's going to short-circuit all the power from here to Pine Hill with that thing," Polly remarked.

"She's got a heavy date tonight," Kate said. "Why are these cards so sticky? You can't even discard. They keep coming back."

It was one of those afternoons. Even Polly's eyes were at half-mast, though she was winning. Then a shadow fell across the floor. We looked up, and Trav was standing out on the porch. Kate scooted her chair back so fast, it nearly went over, and then he was pulling the screen door open and coming in, carrying some packages.

I was amazed. He practically filled up the doorframe. He looked taller, too, a lot, and his shoulders were wider. And his jaw was squarer or something, and he had a deep, reddish tan. He was wearing a wrinkled shirt—Trav in a wrinkled shirt? The sleeves were rolled up high, and he was sprouting hair on his arms. It was a new version of Trav, mature and muscled. He even needed a haircut. Only the horn-rims were the same. He stood there grinning at us, and Polly threw up her hands. The cards went all over.

Kate moved up on him, grabbed him around the neck, and I was on my feet. He had to shift his packages onto the floor to shake my hand. Then we had our arms around each other's shoulders. The three of us hung in there together. Boy, it was good to see him.

"Not a line all summer," Kate said, pounding on him. "Not even a postcard."

"No postcards where I was," he said.

That slowed us down a little. We thought maybe he'd been in some facility-type place. We'd been thinking it all summer.

"I was on my father's cousin's farm. Rural Iowa. Very rural. Not postcard country."

He eased away from us and headed for Polly. He even walked different, and you could see these muscles in his back rippling through the shirt. It was incredible.

"We ought to go looking for Skeeter," I said. "Trav could whip his—"

"Please, Buck," Kate said, but her eyes weren't on me.

He leaned down and gave Polly a big hug, practically lifting her out of the chair. He really held on to her, and she held him. It was a very mellow scene.

Then we were sitting around the table, sort of drinking us in.

"It is really good to see you people," Trav said. "All I've been looking at is cows." He was stretched out in the chair with his hands clasped behind his head. He didn't even sit the same. "So what's been happening? What are the little flags doing up in the orchard?"

Kate looked at Polly. "Oh, I sold it off." Polly made a fanning gesture in the air. "Couldn't be bothered with it anymore."

Maybe he glanced at Kate, maybe not.

"Did right well out of the deal," Polly said, pursing up her mouth. "Had a good lawyer acting for me. It was your daddy, Trav."

His smile faded a little. "My father helped you sell

the orchard?" he said, and Polly nodded. This was news to me too. Kate was looking down in her lap.

"Well, that's great if it's what you want." He turned from Polly to me. After a moment, he said, "Are they going to build right down to your trailer, Buck?"

"Dad and I are going to have to find another hookup anyway," I said, "one of these days. Irene's selling out at the Sunoco."

The changes were piling up. Trav's face clouded up a little. "What does Scotty have to say about that?"

"Hoo-boy," Polly whispered under her breath.

"Scotty's not here," I said. "Scotty got killed, in a robbery."

Trav didn't even really know Scotty, but his eyes went blank behind the horn-rims. He pulled back from that. I thought he pulled too far back.

"My dad and I were pallbearers. Dad's taken it pretty hard. They were really close, the three of them, Scotty and Irene and Dad. They were really tight."

Trav looked aside. "I'm out of touch. My parents only sent me cheery messages."

"What did you send back to them?" Kate said suddenly.

Trav's eyebrows rose. "Cheery messages." Then he brought the smile back. "What's the matter with me? I've forgotten I brought you people presents."

He swung over to the door and scooped up the packages. Two of them were in sacks, but one was in fancy gift wrap. He handed it to Polly.

She made short work of the ribbon and paper and pulled out a bottle of perfume. Lily of the valley.

"Ain't that nice?" Polly said. "That's real thoughtful."

"They're not big on gift items in rural Iowa," Trav said, "so I picked it up in a store here."

He looked around at us, and his grin went out of shape. "I don't mean I picked it up. I mean I bought it."

"Trav," Kate said, "don't—"

"No, it's okay. That's all behind me now. It was just an . . . episode. I had to come back in the middle of the summer, just for a couple of days. I had to see my probation officer. We had a little talk. No charges brought, no court dates. No problem." He glanced over at Polly. "I had your lawyer," he said.

"So, Buck, here's yours." He handed me something flat in a sack. I reached in and pulled out a pocket calculator, a really good one, silver-sided. State-of-the-art.

"I was kind of figuring on electing out of math this year," I said. I turned the calculator over in my hand and saw it wasn't new. I recognized it. It was Trav's, always there in his shirt pocket, practically a part of him till you didn't notice it. He was still smiling. "Maybe I'll take another shot at math," I said. "Maybe this'll get me through."

Actually, I didn't know what to say. But now he was handing a tall sack across the table to Kate. She pulled out a big stuffed toy. It was a Paddington Bear, somewhat dog-eared. It had been Trav's. We'd seen it

in his room, preserved from when he was a kid. Kate
was holding the bear, looking down at it. Her hair fell
forward, and you couldn't see her face.

"You said you had one," Trav said. "So here's another one to keep it company."

"I don't have mine anymore. The stuffing came out
of it or something, a long time ago."

"So now you have a replacement." Trav's grin was
too bright, stretched too tight. There was something
wrong with that moment. Polly's hand crept up to
her lips.

Kate held up the bear. "I'll give it a good home,
Trav." Then she put it away under the table out of
sight. Trav settled in his chair, more laid back than
ever.

"School tomorrow," Kate said, very brisk. "Orientation, registration, the usual pandemonium."

That sort of surprised me. Trav was always so
clenched up about starting school. Now he seemed
totally relaxed, so why bring it up?

But it didn't bother him. It didn't even touch him.
"No problem," he said. "Absolutely no problem."

That first day of school was world-class chaos. We
did nothing but fill out forms and stand in lines for
things like student activity cards. We had red tape up
to here, and we never got around to registration that
day.

Maybe Trav knew we wouldn't. I only caught a
glimpse of him heading someplace after school. He

looked busy, involved. I must have thought he had a club meeting. I don't know what I thought.

The next morning we got around to registration for classes. I was standing in one line in the gym, and Kate was standing in the next one over. She was looking very good that day.

Mr. Handelsman, her drama teacher, came up. You could tell he'd been looking for her. He pulled her out of line.

"Kate, they've had a call at the office and sent me to find you. You're to go home."

She pulled away from him and froze. "You know a boy named Buck Mendenhall?" he said.

"That's me."

Mr. Handelsman turned around. "Oh, good. Buck, will you go home with Kate. Listen, I could take you both in my car."

"No." Kate reached for me, and we cut out running, weaving around the lines in the gym, out the emergency exit. She ran like a deer and didn't even slow down till we were nearly to her lane. I was winded before she was.

"It's Polly," she said. "I'm sure of it." She kicked a sizable stone into the ditch. "I'm not ready for this."

I didn't say anything. I thought it was Polly too. We were crunching up their lane. Kate got as far as the back porch step. But she had to take hold of the railing to make herself go on. When she pulled open the screen door, I was as close behind her as I could be.

Polly was sitting there in her chair. You could still

smell the breakfast coffee. It was a completely ordinary morning, except it wasn't. Dad was standing beside Polly's chair. My dad was there.

I thought Kate would make a run for Polly, but she stopped. Her sneaker skidded on the linoleum, and she pulled back against me. Polly was looking aside, and her hand was up at her cheek.

"You children come in and sit down," she said, not even looking at us.

We sat down at the kitchen table, and it was too big for the two of us. Dad came over and stood between our chairs. Polly stayed back.

"We have something we have to tell you," Dad said. "But you want to remember we're here together. We're right here for each other."

Kate put her hand up to stop him, but she let it rest down on the table. I memorized the wood grain around her hand.

"This morning, when the crew came to work to start cleaning out the orchard, they found Trav there."

Kate's fingers curled. Her nails dug into the wood.

"There's a little clearing in there, and . . . that's where he was."

"Yes," Kate said, quick. "We go down there. Well, we haven't lately, but we used to. Buck knows the place, don't you, Buck? I don't know what we'll do without it." She jerked her head away and looked out the window like she could see the clearing from there.

"Kate." Dad's hand just brushed my arm when he

reached down to brace himself on the table. "Trav got confused in his mind. He took . . . He died."

I heard Dad's voice above me, every word, but I was down in some pit where it echoed.

She was still looking away. She reached up to cover her ears, but her hands stopped short.

"I have to tell you this. You have to hear me out. When they found him, they had to cut him down."

I thought of the collar, the high World War I uniform collar around Trav's neck.

Kate's head whipped around. Her eyes bored holes in Dad. "Cut?"

"He'd . . . tied a rope around a limb. They couldn't do anything for him."

"They couldn't do anything for him," Kate repeated in an echo. "Oh, I know. He never will let you do anything for him. He's like that. But he's all right now, isn't he?"

"Oh, child," Polly said behind us.

Dad's hand closed tight over my shoulder, and I remembered him at the police station with Trav. I thought I was Trav, and all we'd need to do is sign some papers for the chief and leave.

"We lost him," Dad said. "Trav killed himself."

Kate's eyes were gray and dry. "Then he's all right. He's safe." She nodded and then looked straight at me. "But what about us?"

We lived through the morning. Kate would start to get up but sit down again. Once she got as far as the cupboard and started taking things out. I guess she was going to clean it, but she came back and sat down again. You could look at her hands and see how cold they were.

But she never left the room. We all stayed together. I wouldn't have turned my back on any of them for fear another of us would be gone. I sat there beside my dad until my mind went back to when I was a little kid, the way I used to sit next to him in the cab of whatever truck he was driving. I'd sit so close, he didn't have elbow room to shift gears. But I'd hang in there by him, and nothing could get me.

Along about noon I saw Kate try to reach down in herself and pull up some anger. I'd seen her do that before.

"Why didn't we say something? I'm talking to you, Buck. People don't pay any attention to kids, but why didn't we make them hear?"

"We didn't know," I said with my head down.

"We should have. Think back and you'll see."

I couldn't take much more, but I was too dry inside to cry. "They were little things."

"They added up," Kate said, "and they weren't little. The poem, the pear trees poem. Even that. Remember that? They weren't little things. Why didn't we have someplace—somebody to go to to tell us what they meant?"

"I should have knowed," Polly said, hollow, behind us.

"No!" Kate's hand reached out in the air between them. "Not you, Polly. I didn't mean you." That was the only time all day that Kate sounded like Kate. "You were like us, Polly. Too close. Too close."

"I should have knowed," Polly said, not hearing. "But you were all so young."

Now I was reaching down inside myself for anything I could find. "When he came back the other day," I said, "he seemed better. He looked great. He was better." I saw us there together day before yesterday in this same kitchen. These walls, those calendars.

"No he wasn't," Kate said. "He gave us those presents because he wouldn't need them anymore. Buck, he was saying good-bye. And we were deaf people. We were blind."

She looked around, and I knew she was looking for a solution. She loved solutions. She was looking for a way out, a way back. She looked all over: on the windowsills, in the cupboard with its door still standing open. It wasn't there.

"I'll tell you one thing," she said in a low voice, cold. "I'll grow up, but I'll never trust anything again. I'll never believe in anything or anybody. You can count on that."

It was noontime quiet. The kitchen was half dark, and the idiot sun was streaming in and the maniac flies were buzzing the screen door. It was a beautiful day. Why is it in your memories it's never raining?

Then Polly spoke. "I have lived too long," she said.

CHAPTER FIFTEEN

They didn't have a funeral for Trav or bury him here. Mr. and Mrs. Kirby took him back to someplace they'd lived before for that. In a way it was a mistake. A funeral would have satisfied a lot of people who get off on death, a lot of people around school. A lot of people who think they can't die.

The next day Kate and I went back to school together. Where else were we supposed to be? She came down to the trailer early. She'd never done that before because it was out of her way. I wasn't even dressed yet, but she waited outside. When I came out, she was standing at the edge of Irene's weedy garden, wearing an old Windbreaker and skirt. They looked like the first things she'd reached for.

We were out on the county road when I said, "I'd have stopped by for you."

"I just wanted to be sure," she said. Then we were passing the road they'd cut into the orchard. It dawned on me that she'd had to walk past it by herself, coming for me. It was only a couple of ruts, but yellow clay tire tracks led out of it onto the blacktop. I thought once we got past them, we'd be over the worst.

It was the first day of classes, so things were hectic anyway, but word was around about Trav, and everybody in school was an expert. In a way it was ironic. Trav turned out to be a unifying force, and we'd never had one before. You could yell *"Fire!"* in that school, and most people would think it didn't apply to them. But now they all owned Trav. They replayed him on their Betamax brains. They had him for breakfast, with leftovers for lunch.

When Kate and I came into the halls, they made way for us, created space around us. Their faces were long, and they were loving it. Girls stood around crying, and they'd never even met Trav. Guys stood in bunches, discussing knots.

"I don't accept this," Kate murmured. "I don't accept any of this."

It started in a low hum, and built. Finally, everybody had been Trav's best friend, and everybody had known all along he was crazy. As for Kate and me, if it had been yearbook time, everybody would have wanted us to sign theirs.

I tried not to be there. Every day I tried to send my body off to school and be there when it came home. So did Kate. It worked for a while.

In the first week Trav was a hot topic. He won out over orientation, registration, taming new teachers.

In the second week you began to hear about this

entirely new Trav, this revised version. He was an alcoholic glue-sniffer with a brain tumor, malignant.

By the third week I thought it was getting better for me, now that they weren't dissecting anybody I'd ever known. In fourth-period Biology II, I'd have my daily fantasy. It seemed like Kate and Trav were having lunch together while I was stuck in class. Seems like we never all get to have lunch together anymore. I had a jab of the old jealousy, and it felt good.

They wouldn't let it go, though. They wanted to talk about it in classes, and teachers let them. Word got around that killing yourself can turn into an epidemic, can really spread. People began looking at Kate and me with whole new eyes.

Around then, somebody got up in history class and said we ought to have a day of mourning for Trav. We ought to close school, and it got a big round of applause from the same people who like snow days.

Word finally penetrated to the administration. I guess teachers told them they weren't getting anything else done in class. They decided they'd better hold a public meeting with parents and students and all interested community members. They decided they had a problem on their hands. They printed up a mailing piece and sent it out.

Kate said she wouldn't go. She and I walked to school together and home again at night, but that was it. She'd pulled back inside herself. She waited in there because she didn't even have the orchard clearing to go down to now.

When Dad got the mailing piece, he said, "We're going."

"Why?" I said. "What's the point?"

"Because it might help. I don't like how you're taking this. You're hurting, and you're not giving yourself enough trouble about it. You're not giving me enough trouble."

So we had to go. It was on a school night, scheduled in the auditorium where Trav and I hadn't seen Kate in *The Glass Menagerie.* But the place was too big. There was this handful of people dotted around the auditorium in separate spaces: forty of them, tops. Quite a few teachers, a few kids, a scattering of other people—parents, maybe. The administration was there in force, milling around on the stage. They almost outnumbered us. Finally they decided to adjourn us to the student lounge, which would be more the right size.

I heard Trav's voice in my mind, clear as a bell, commenting on this move. "The administration is into group dynamics," he said, "like seating configuration and room size. They learn these things at seminars."

Dad and I went down the halls with the other people, and then, walking along beside us, was a woman who had a little baby with her. She carried it in a sling over one shoulder. It was Sherrie Slater. She looked wonderful, and her baby was about the size of a doll, sound asleep in its sling with a pacifier in its mouth.

"Hello, Buck," she said.

It was a strange thing. My arm went out around her shoulder, and I hugged her. At the same time she put her arm around me. With her other hand she held her baby steady, and we never stopped walking. It was okay: She wasn't our teacher anymore.

"I came tonight because of her." Sherrie looked down at her baby, and I saw it was wearing a little pink knitted thing. "Having a baby changes you. I never was much of a teacher, but I really want to be a great mother. I want her to grow up and be happy. And I want to know when she isn't. So I came here tonight."

Sherrie spoke in her same breathy voice. But the before I could introduce her and Dad or think abou it, she moved on ahead in her flat-heeled shoes and her loose dress and her baby in a sling.

Then we were in the student lounge in these molded plastic chairs, and the place smelled like dead cigarette butts. We were closer together in there, sitting closer at least. More people came. Mr. and Mrs. Kirby came in.

It seemed like a coincidence to me. I'd been working on a new fantasy about them. Mr. and Mrs. Kirby had pulled Trav out of school for a Bermuda vacation. But when I saw them in the lounge, they had no tans, and it was just the two of them.

That brought me halfway back to reality. I remembered Mr. Kirby was president of the school board.

The administration had set up a row of chairs facing ours, and they were leading the Kirbys up to them, but they were shaking their heads. Instead, they sat down in the front with the rest of us.

"Now it's going to be like a funeral. Now we have to have that."

Dad looked at me. "Whatever works."

The assistant principal got up, a youngish guy who coaches the tennis team on the side. He had on a summer suit. He cleared his throat and looked around for the mike that wasn't there.

"We're here this evening as a community concerned about our young people." He looked out over us, counting the concerned. A lot of Trav's chief mourners around school were missing, but then, this wasn't on school time.

But ahead of Dad and me, down the row, I caught a glimpse of Rusty Hazenfield. She was sitting by herself, and as I saw her she turned and saw me. She just raised her hand, a little signal. She didn't make big eyes or give out one of her sunflower smiles.

"Our community has been struck by a problem of growing proportions around the country. We are not immune. Young people today are taking their own lives in record numbers. It's a senseless pattern of destruction, and it strikes at some of our most promising youth."

I could see the backs of Mr. and Mrs. Kirby's heads. Hers was up, firm. His was bent.

"This is a community problem. No school, however

caring and compassionate, is equipped to cope with a problem essentially rooted in home and family."

Mr. Kirby's head began to rise. But now there was a sound at the back of the room, something scraping against the frame of the door. I looked back and saw Kate, and her mom was with her. Polly was there too. They were working her wheelchair through the door. Polly was looking around, her glasses flashing. You could just see her between the heads of other people as Kate and her mom got the wheelchair inside, at the back.

"The death of a promising student has affected every member of the student body. On the academic level, it's been a distraction at a crucial time in the school year. We administrators are keenly aware that one suicide can lead to more. As administrators, our job is to keep our fingers on the pulse of the young."

I was hearing everything he said, and I didn't even know his name. I didn't know he had his finger on my pulse. I looked down at the inside of my wrist.

"We see how teenagers get caught up in what essentially can be a fad. We see it, but there is no mechanism to inform young people of the finality of death, that suicide is a permanent solution to a temporary problem."

He eased a little, now that he was rolling. He hiked up his seersucker coat and put his hand down in his pant pocket. "We've provided the facilities for the meeting this evening even though the young man we thought so much of did not take his life on school property. We're here because young people who feel heavily pressured by the expectations of their parents can crack under the strain. We're here to turn over this problem to the community in hope of positive feedback."

He looked back at his boss, the principal, who nodded.

There was a moment of silence, now that the meeting was thrown open to the public: us, I guess. Then Mr. Kirby was getting to his feet, moving like an old man.

"I yield the floor to Mr. Kirby, president of the school board and . . . parent," the assistant principal said.

When Mr. Kirby turned to face us, I saw Trav again: the long thin face, the square jaw, the straight line of the mouth. The intelligence. He stood there turning into Trav, and I went back a year, remembering the good times.

I remembered that time last year when Kate and Trav liberated me from freshman football. I heard Trav saying, "It's pretty time-consuming, and we'd miss having you around. It wouldn't be the same."

I heard it word for word before Mr. Kirby began to speak in his own, lawyer voice.

"I have listened to the assistant principal here in this school, where our son has distinguished himself as a student."

Mr. Kirby's hand came up to hold on to something, but it was only air. He looked behind himself at the administration in a row.

"You have called me a parent. I no longer am. That

was taken from me and from my wife. We're parents without a child. God spare anyone else in this room that fate.

"This evening I've heard from the assistant principal that the school assumes no responsibility for our son. I hear the annoyance in the assistant principal's voice that Trav's death has caused academic disruption. I hear the relief in his voice that our boy didn't die on school property.

"My wife and I hear that this death is our fault, that we pushed our son over the edge to his death. Yet, we've watched him come home from this school day after day, unfulfilled and hungry for a challenge he wasn't getting in even the advanced classes. He didn't believe this school was preparing him for the future. He grew . . . desperate."

Mrs. Kirby's head began to lower. He saw that and finished up.

"I tender my resignation as president of the school board. I have nothing more to offer, and nothing left to lose. I wish I could reach out to you people who have come here tonight, but I don't know how. We aren't a community. We are all strangers here."

He went over to Mrs. Kirby then, wooden, soldierly. He took her hand and helped her stand and led her away. At the door she smiled and nodded to people, and you knew she didn't really understand where she was. Then they were gone.

People wanted to leave then. Chairs scraped. But coming up the side of the room past us was Polly, working the wheels of her chair. She came to the front and turned the chair neatly toward us. People leaned forward to see her.

She let them look while the light played on her pink scalp. Then she spoke in her hollow voice, crystal clear in the room.

"Oh, yes, I'm as old as I look. My name's Polly Prior, and I've lived here in Slocum Township all my life. I don't get out much now. Well, you see how I am."

Her hands thumped the chrome arms of her chair.

"I had a brother once—Harold. You wouldn't remember him. He went off to the First War, and he never come back. I don't mourn him anymore, but I keep him by me in my mind."

People looked away from her, ready to be embarrassed.

"And now we've lost another young boy, and not in a war, not in foreign parts. He just slipped away from us, didn't he? And his folks blame the school, and the school blames his folks.

"That lets the rest of us off scot-free, don't it? There's people here who come tonight to hear how a problem was going to be handled for them. There's young ones who want all the responsibility put on the grown-ups. And there's grown ones here who say it can't happen to people like us. There's people in this room who come to slake their curiosity about a crazy boy, to hear how crazy he was so they'll think they're sane enough to be safe.

"Trav Kirby was a boy troubled in his mind. I been

troubled in my mind many a time. If that makes me a crazy woman, you better lock me up."

She gazed around the room. She had a way of looking everybody square in the eye.

"Maybe there's some people here who come to find out what they could do, to educate themselves.

"Children hide themselves from their parents, and parents let them. School administrators hide from themselves, and taxpayers pay them to do it.

"Maybe there's teachers in this room who will show their students the warning signs. Maybe there's young people here who'd rather care about their living schoolmates than spread rumors about their dead ones. We cannot have a community until we are ready to be one.

"I'm old and don't know. I don't know many of you out there. When I was a child, I played in the fields where you live now. But I won't tell you how things was back then. Maybe I don't remember rightly. Maybe I only remember the good times."

Polly's mouth worked in silence for a moment, and people waited, respectful.

"That boy who died was right smart in many ways. Handsome, too, and gentle in his ways. He put me in mind of my brother, Harold.

"He had parents who thought he was perfect and friends who loved him. Maybe he didn't love himself enough, but he was loved. I loved him. He was like one of my own. There's a girl in this room who's lost without him. There's a boy in this room still hunting him in his heart."

She paused and nobody breathed.

"I wonder if, when Trav went, he took a part of that girl and that boy with him. I hope he didn't take too much, for I cannot do without them. I'm old, you see, and selfish."

She waited again. She was waiting for something—some response.

I heard another sound then, far off. It was a sob, coming up hard. I heard it break. I heard a wail and weeping. And boy, was I glad, because Kate had held too much inside herself too long.

Then I looked down at the front of my shirt, and it was wet already. And it was my sob and my wail and my weeping. But it was too late to stop.

Why should I? I broke open, and I cried for us all.

I didn't know where I was, but I knew Kate was crying too. She was back there with her mom, and her mom was there for her. But somehow I heard Kate over the sound of myself. I heard her in my heart.

People were looking, or looking away. People had their hands up to their faces and over their eyes. People reached out and touched. Somehow I saw through a blur. From the corner of my mind, I wondered if something might be beginning.

When I could, when I could swallow, I said to Dad, "This won't bring him back."

Dad's arm was around me, and his head was thrown back, but his shirt was wet too. "No," he said. "This brings you back."

SPRINGTIME

O r trying to be. And I'm not remembering now, because in your memories it's never raining, and it's raining today. March rain's hosing down the last of the parking-lot snowpiles and greening up the ground. Rain's falling at a slant, warmer than the steaming earth.

We're sixteen now, Kate and I. This is no time to tell you about the new driver's license burning a hole in my pocket. Or about the spring play that Kate's directing. She's decided that she's a born director, and I could have told her that all along.

But you just about have to take a number to get near her. Most evenings, almost every evening, I hang around outside the auditorium, waiting for her to get out of rehearsal.

Kate came out of the stage door a little while ago and said they'd just be five minutes more.

And now here she is, looking good. Her eyebrows so fine they almost aren't there, and her gray eyes spotting me. And her perfect mouth—complaining.

"Why are we putting on a musical?" she's saying,

"and why am I even involved in it? And why does no high school boy want to admit he's a tenor when we need tenors?"

Since it's raining, she pulls on her yellow plastic poncho with the hood, and I turn up the collar on my jacket for all the good it will do. We start off across the field, and the grass is practically jumping up out of the ground, and it smells like—

"The pear trees all in bloom," Kate says. "Remember Trav's poem?"

I remember. "I wish—"

"So do I," Kate says, and there's more than raindrops on her lashes.

"Boy, I love that guy," I say.

"So do I," Kate says, taking my arm, and we run.

And Polly? I wouldn't leave you wondering. Polly's still with us. She's the third oldest woman in Slocum Township, but when it comes to meanness, she's Number One.